MW00905289

THE WICKED GAME OF THE HUNTER SERIES, BOOK #1

WICKED GAME
—— · —— OF THE —— · ——
HUNTER

TRACEY L. RYAN

LUMINARE PRESS

WWW.LUMINAREPRESS.COM

Wicked Game of the Hunter
Copyright © 2016 Tracey L. Ryan
Revised May 2020

All rights reserved. No part of this book may be reproduced, scanned, or distributed in any printed or electronic form without the prior written permission of the author/publisher.

This is a work of fiction. Names, characters, places, and incidents either are the product of the author's imagination or are used fictitiously and any resemblance to actual persons, living or dead, businesses, companies, or locales is entirely coincidental.

Printed in the United States of America

LCCN: 2017904614
ISBN: 9781544794044

To my father who always supported me with unconditional love in my many endeavors and will be eternally missed.

Prologue

Five Years Earlier

Dusk was fast approaching the small, Norman Rockwell-style town of Hardwicke. The snow was falling at about an inch an hour as the golden winter sun set over the hills that surrounded the town like sentries guarding a palace. Although the middle-aged man drove as slowly as possible in four-wheel drive, the winding roads were starting to get slicker. Not surprisingly, the plows still hadn't made their way this far out of town yet. What started out as a gloriously beautiful January day had ultimately turned into a potentially treacherous evening.

The man was thankful to have the Jeep Grand Cherokee tonight when he drove down for milk at the nearest store, which was four miles away from his home. His pride and joy would *not* be happy to know he used the last of it, and she wouldn't have any for her morning tea. His thoughts drifted to work and his recent discovery. If what he thinks he found is the real deal, it will change the medical world forever. The man decided to leave another message for his employer in hopes they could speak tonight when he got home. The competition in this market was fierce—every minute counted.

In the near distance, the man saw headlights coming toward him and slowed the Jeep to almost a crawl as both vehicles approached the hairpin turn on Old Ravine Road. His thoughts drifted back to work. Why hadn't his employer returned his call yet? Although the cell reception was sometimes sporadic, he hoped that his employer received the message—it was so unlike him not to call back. In fact, his employer was a micro-manager to the point of being absurd. He usually stayed in the city in bad weather, but his employer was hounding him to work from home with the pending snowstorm instead—which was very odd behavior. But he didn't argue because that meant he could spend more time with his daughter, the apple of his eye, who was home from college.

The man brought his thoughts back to driving in the fast deteriorating conditions. This road, perfectly serene in the good weather as it overlooked the tranquil houses down below, was downright murderous in the winter months with its countless accidents into the ravine. Hardwicke was one of those rare places that still possessed all its natural beauty. Even the snow seemed to glisten in a mystical way that could only be seen far away from any city influence. There was a purity about the town

Tracey L. Ryan

that only its inhabitants could truly understand and appreciate.

He remembered when his daughter saw the snow fall for the first time. They had the fireplace on in the living room and were sitting on the couch reading to her. She was a little peanut at six months old but had a world's worth of curiosity already in her. She became mesmerized as soon as the perfectly white flakes started to fall outside the window next to the couch. He had known even before she was born that she was special and destined for greatness.

The high beam headlights of the other vehicle were now directly in his view and almost blinding him, snapping him out of his nostalgia. The other driver must not know the road or somehow hadn't see him. The man gripped the steering wheel a little tighter. He flashed his lights, but it looked like the other car was going to hit him head-on. He tried to swerve. The road was narrow and without guardrails. There was nowhere for him to go. The Jeep's tires rattled dangerously close to the edge of the embankment that led down to the ravine. Why wasn't the other car returning to their lane? Must be a drunk driver, the man immediately thought.

The Jeep started to fishtail. As the front tires hit the snow-covered gravel on the edge of the road it spun 180 degrees. It teetered and started to go over. The vehicle lost any remaining balance and rolled over on its driver's side, then again onto its roof while it continued to slide down the embankment. Glass shattered like confetti at a birthday party as the metal made an unnerving crunch sound. The Jeep's driver's seatbelt became unhooked. He was tossed around the front seat of the vehicle as it virtually collapsed around him. Only the steering wheel prevented him from being thrown out of the vehicle where the front windshield used to be.

The seconds felt like an eternity for the driver as the Jeep tumbled downward. A large boulder brought it to a stop at the bottom of the ravine. What used to be the front-end of the Jeep was now melded with the boulder so that it looked like an abstract piece of art. The engine hissed as smoke poured out, shrouding the Jeep in a white and grey cloak.

When the world stopped moving, the man was semi-conscious. Not quite in this world but not in the next either. In his last moments before heading to the great beyond, his only thoughts were of his precious daughter.

Although he knew no one would hear him, he whispered, "I love you, Punkin." Then eternal darkness fell on him and all his secrets were forever hidden as the snow gently covered the vehicle in a plush, white blanket.

The dark SUV that idled on the road at the top of the ravine for a few more moments. Then the passenger rolled down the window. The air started to smell like gasoline. The passenger threw their still lit Macanudo cigar down into the ravine. Satisfied that there was no movement in the vehicle at the bottom, the passenger signaled the driver. SUV drove away unnoticed as the Jeep burst into flames.

CHAPTER 1

Emma Sharpeton was nothing less than stunning with her slight frame, lustrous shoulder-length, naturally honey-blonde hair, and exotic, emerald green eyes. Today she chose to wear a new grey pinstriped Calvin Klein pant suit with a light pink camisole and black Etienne Aigner pumps. Spring had finally sprung in the energized city of Boston as she walked to her marketing consulting firm from her two-bedroom condo on the waterfront.

Emma had founded Sharpeton Consulting only three years ago and already it was being recognized as one of the fastest growing small firms owned by a woman. She has always had a mind for business. After she received her MBA from Harvard she took a huge risk starting her own company fresh out of college. Even in high school, she tended to choose books over boys, something she began to regret as she got older, especially the one boy who broke her heart.

Tracey L. Ryan

Normally, Mondays were tough to get back into the swing of work after the weekend's adventures, but today was a day to celebrate. Her team didn't know it yet, but the firm had been awarded the marketing contract for the annual Children's Hospital Gala event. This would help elevate her company to the next level in both the business and marketing worlds.

Emma arrived at her building and stopped outside the front door to soak in the city for a minute. Boston was a city full of energy, resilience, and perseverance. Most people Emma's age loved the nightlife, but she came alive in the early morning watching the businesspeople rushing to get their caffeine-fix before heading to their offices. Newspaper vendors hawked the latest local and national tidbits as taxis maneuvered around the throngs of early risers.

Emma entered the building on High Street and was warmly greeted by the building's security guard. Stan was a retired Boston police officer happily living out his later years by enjoying the slow lane. He was a tall man of 6'5," in his early 60s with thick grey hair, and some extra girth proving how much he enjoyed his wife's cooking.

"Good morning, Ms. Sharpeton. Beautiful morning, isn't it?"

"Good morning, Stan. It's a picture-perfect day in the city. Hope you can get out there and enjoy some of it," Emma said with her usual contagious smile.

"Hoping to bring the grandkids to Boston Common for some ice cream," Stan said in his thick Boston accent. "Maybe one of these days take the family on one of those trolley tours. Lived here all my life and I've never been on one of those darn things," he added with a chuckle and smiled.

The elevator doors opened as Emma waved goodbye to Stan, flashing yet another smile. She thought about how her father would have said something like that. Emma pressed the button for the sixth floor, home of Sharpeton Consulting. Although the building is one of the older ones in the neighborhood, the elevator was recently upgraded so the ride up to the top floor was relatively smooth. Emma chose this building to be her headquarters because it was one of the few buildings that still held its original Victorian charm. The original hard wood floors and brick façade dated from the late-1800s.

The elevator doors slowly opened and Emma stepped into the foyer of the modern yet traditional looking office space. When designing the space, she tried to keep as much of the charm as possible while offering her staff the elegant sophistication of mahogany and floor-to-ceiling glass. The space allowed for a small reception area, five glass-enclosed offices, two conference rooms and ample open cube space. The design was to reflect collaboration and creativity while still providing the staff with their own personal space.

Emma had only taken two steps out of the elevator and into the reception area before her receptionist, Ashley, practically tackled her.

"Emma, you won't guess who called and wants to do a story on you! You will absolutely die when you find out! I mean, it's incredible!"

Emma interrupted her rant, trying not to show her irritation. "Ashley, I won't find out if you don't take a breath and tell me."

"Oh, sorry. You know I get a little excitable sometimes. Wendy Aucoin from the Boston Times called and wants to do a feature on you and the firm for the Sunday business section. They are featuring the fastest growing start-ups in the Bay State. Isn't that awesome?" Ashley said, grinning like a puppy wanting a treat from its owner.

Emma froze like a statue except for her mouth dropping open. For the first time in a long time she was speechless. This wasn't like being on a TV talk show, but a major metropolitan newspaper wanted to feature her company for an article. It was intimidating and exhilarating at the same time. This could be the start of the next chapter for her professional life—it would showcase her and the company to the world, or at least to those who read the local paper.

"Emma, you aren't going to pass out or anything are you? Should I get you some water? You look a little pale."

"Thanks. I'm fine—just…just a little shocked. Leave me Wendy's contact information. I'll call her back later today. I just need a few minutes in my office before we start the staff meeting."

"Aye, aye, Captain!" Ashley said as she danced back to her desk to answer the phone.

Emma retreated to the semi-solitude of her corner office. The glass walls and floor-to-ceiling windows sometimes made her feel like she was in a fishbowl, but the expansive view was one that most only dreamed of having at work. And something this small-town girl from Hardwicke, a town most had never heard of, worked for in spades.

Every Monday morning, Emma insisted they hold a staff meeting to review the projects for the week, any challenges, and the chance to brainstorm. She intended to completely surprise the team and have a little fun with them at the same time.

She could hear her fifteen employees gathering in the central conference room. Chairs were being moved, coffee mugs were clanking on the mahogany table, and low chatter about people's weekends was taking place. At precisely 9 a.m., Emma made her way down the hall to the conference room, trying to put on a somber façade. She opened the glass door. The chatter came to an abrupt halt and everyone looked up at her. She knew her expression was an award-winning performance as she was doing cart-wheels inside. Emma knew what this contract meant to every person at the table. This was the first time the company was going to be on the same playing field as other more mature marketing firms. And not only on the same playing field, they scored the winning goal.

"I hope everyone had a good weekend." She paused. "I know everyone worked very hard over the last several weeks on the proposal for the Children's Hospital Gala event, and I want everyone to know how much I appreciate your efforts. As you know, the committee was to make a decision this weekend, and they did. They called me on Saturday morning to announce their decision."

She could see her employees' smiles turning into frowns. The excitement in the room only moments before had been perfectly deflated. It was all she could do to stop herself from chuckling. Yes, they would probably run her over on the street for fooling them like this, but it was going to be priceless.

"I want you to know that the committee thought we provided a valiant effort. They did, however, receive many outstanding proposals. Please know that just being asked to provide a proposal for something of this stature is a reward in itself and an honor that we should be proud of."

Not one person sitting at the table could anticipate what was about to happen. "So, you should all give yourselves a pat on the back for a job well-done. And congratulate yourselves…for *winning* the Children's Hospital Gala contract! You did it! We won!"

Emma beamed a very smug smile as she walked over to the cabinet-style refrigerator along the conference room wall to open several bottles of Biutiful champagne from Spain, which she had hidden there on Sunday. It took a few seconds for the news to completely register with people and then the jubilation began. She was the first one to shake the bottle of champagne and spray the team with it as they were screaming, crying, and high-fiving each other.

"Ashley, can you help me pour the champagne and pass it out to the team?"

Ashley, unusually speechless, started pulling out the Mikasa crystal champagne glasses etched with the company logo.

"While Ashley is passing out the glasses, I want you to know how extremely proud I am of this team. This was a huge win for our firm, and one that couldn't have been accomplished without the hard work of *every single person* in this room. So, here's to you! Cheers! Salute!"

The whole room sounded like a symphony of crystal as glasses clanked and the team cheered and hugged each other. Emma just smiled as she watched the team enjoy their moment. They all knew that this was an incredible opportunity for the firm and for each of them personally. And they all knew it would require countless hours of work over the next two months. Although no one in the room, including Emma, knew the dark domino effect that was about to happen as a result of this project.

"Although it pains me to break up our little celebration, we need to start working through the logistics for this campaign, so please, everyone, take your seats."

The team quickly got back to their seats and finished up what remained in each of their glasses. Everyone in the room took out their Microsoft Surface tablets and called up their files so that the discussion could begin.

"We submitted three different campaign styles for the Gala. The committee chose the black and white, simple, sophistication version. I think this will work well given the venue is the headquarters for Ares Logan Industries."

The team all let out a gasp - Ares Logan Industries was on the Forbes Top 50 List and had clients all over the world. The building itself had been featured in over half a dozen architectural design magazines for its modern design, 30-story lobby atrium with a real park and koi pond in the center, and rose-hued glass showing off its architectural elegance.

Emma hoped that no one at the table remembered that she had grown up with the CEO and owner of the conglomerate, Hunter Logan. Her thoughts drifted back to growing up in Hardwicke and horseback riding with Hunter. Even at 15-years-old, anyone who saw him knew he was going to grow up to be devilishly handsome. Hunter's family owned a large estate off the center of town with stables for up to six horses. His father loved to ride so he had ensured that the entire family learned to ride. The family divided their time between Hardwicke, Boston, and London, depending on Phillip Logan's business obligations. Emma had spent a great deal of time over Hunter's house when he was in Hardwicke, creating a bond that not many understood given their very different backgrounds. Hunter came from a privileged family of considerable wealth, grew up in boarding schools in London, and had been groomed to take over his family's interests almost from birth. Emma was from a middle-class family, chose public school over private school, and couldn't imagine such a structured life. Even though they were from completely different worlds, Emma had always known that Hunter was her first love.

Emma was quickly brought back to the present. "Emma, didn't you used to know Hunter Logan?" asked their graphic designer, Evan Stewards.

Evan was an extremely talented graphic designer, and Emma was lucky to have him on the team, but he was the biggest office gossip she had ever known. Emma figured it was probably because he basically had no life—all he did was work, read Hollywood gossip blogs, and tend his two cats.

"Yes, Evan, Mr. Logan and I knew each other but that was a lifetime ago. I doubt he even remembers me. It's not like we moved in the same circles." At least Emma hoped Hunter wouldn't remember her. She knew he was sure to be at the Gala. The thought of seeing him after all this time put a knot in her stomach but also excited her for reasons unknown.

The rest of the day was filled with the typical client conference calls and internal meetings. At five o'clock, the office was still full of people buzzing around like a beehive. The office started to have a ginger orange hue as the setting sun reflected off the water. Emma took a moment to look out at her staff, mesmerized by all the creativity that was emanating from the team. An incredible energy seemed to have taken over the team.

She stepped out of her office and, in as commanding a voice she could muster, told everyone to go home for the day. Emma herself couldn't wait to go home, have leftover Chinese food, and slump on the couch to watch *Criminal Minds* re-runs. Living alone had its advantages—she could watch what she wanted and eat what she wanted. She grabbed the reporter's contact information that Ashley had left on her desk along with her other belongings to make the trek home.

CHAPTER 2

———

The walk home was uneventful. The sun was setting, encasing the city in a golden shroud that seemed almost angelic. Dusk was almost as beautiful as sunrise, Emma thought, with the light reflecting off the glass towers that rose above the ocean like the mystical city of Atlantis.

Emma entered her dimly lit penthouse condo on the Boston waterfront a mere fifteen minutes after leaving her office. She had accomplished so much in such a short amount of time, but she sometimes felt an emptiness inside her on nights like this. Her mother would say it was because she didn't have a 'significant other' in her life. She desperately missed being able to share days like this with her father, who had died tragically in a car accident five years ago.

When she got in those moods, Emma would often look at the stars from the vast array of windows in her living room. She always found a single twinkling star and imagined it was her father smiling

Tracey L. Ryan

down on her. Her father had the same contagious smile she did, and she was happy it was one of the many things he passed down to her.

Emma kicked off her shoes in the gourmet kitchen and took the leftover Chinese food out of the oversized refrigerator. She piled pork fried rice, spareribs, and teriyaki strips on a plate and put it in the microwave for a few minutes. As the buzzer went off several times, she realized she hadn't told her mother about the Gala yet. I most definitely need to call her tonight, Emma made a mental note. The wrath of Victoria Sharpeton would be like an F-5 tornado if her mother read about her firm's triumph online before Emma told her.

She poured sweet and sour sauce over the plate of food and went to the living room so she could eat while watching TV. Emma rarely sat in the kitchen or dining room to eat unless she had friends or family over, even though she had spent a small fortune furnishing and decorating the dining room. It had taken her almost three months to find the perfect furniture and color scheme. She finally decided on crisp white walls with a traditional merlot-colored wood dining room table with six matching leather chairs and a matching two-piece china cabinet.

Emma bought the penthouse soon after starting Sharpeton Consulting. It was a deal she couldn't pass up. The previous owners were relocating to

Los Angeles due to a work promotion, so they needed to sell the property quickly. Water's Edge Towers was a perfect amount of luxury without being pretentious. Her living room had views of both the city and the waterfront—benefits of the corner location of the penthouse. Another benefit was that she had a wraparound deck that allowed for outdoor entertaining in good weather.

The two-bedroom, two-bathroom condo had everything Emma ever wanted and then some. There were cherry hardwoods throughout the space, a gourmet kitchen with maple cabinets and stainless-steel Wolf appliances, and a parking garage. Every room afforded her panoramic views of the harbor and city. With a gas fireplace and built-in bar in the living room, what more could a girl ask for?

Emma settled in on the granite-colored chenille couch in front of the 52-inch HD TV. The room was decent size and allowed her to have the sofa plus matching loveseat and chair. Instead of hanging the TV above the fireplace like her brother, Robert, wanted her to do, she had chosen to house it in the espresso-colored entertainment center, which coordinated with the end tables. The room had a contemporary feel to it with the dark wood, granite-colored furniture, and powder blue walls.

Robert had been so upset that she didn't buy a larger TV. She chuckled to herself as she thought of their rather loud, childish argument in the middle of Best Buy. His argument solely was that it wouldn't give her the best sports viewing. Emma had never cared about sports a day in her life! The clincher was when he threw out, "What happens when you bring a guy here and he wants to watch the Bruins or Pats?" At that comment, Emma had shaken her head and walked away thinking guys were all the same.

As she reminisced, she realized how much she missed Robert. She seemed to miss him more and more since their father's death five years ago. Even though he was the typical annoying big brother, he was also the one person who always had her back. Growing up he was always protective of her, but it seemed to take new meaning when their father died. Although Robert was across the pond in London, they still managed to text almost every day, which she was thankful for.

As *Criminal Minds* came on, Emma decided to text Robert to let him know about winning the bid for the Gala. Given the time difference, he probably wouldn't get it until tomorrow morning, but at least he wouldn't be able to tell her he had to see it on the internet first. She finished her dinner then rinsed the single dish and silverware before putting them in the dishwasher.

It was time to call her mother. Victoria had been living in Arizona for the past two years. Three years after her father's death, her mother decided that warmer climates were more for her than the harsh New England winters. The phone rang twice before Victoria picked it up and answered in her usual cheery manner.

"Hello, darling."

"Hi, Mom. How are you?"

"I didn't expect to hear from you tonight. Usually you only call on the weekends. Is everything okay? What's wrong?"

Emma sighed at the typical Mom drama. "Everything is great. I wanted to share my good news with you."

"Oh my God! Are you finally dating someone? Tell me everything!"

"No, I'm not dating anyone. It's about work."

"Oh." Victoria sounded deflated.

"My company won the contract for the Boston Children's Hospital Gala in two months. This is going to be all over the local news. *And*, the Boston Times is running a feature on my company."

"Oh, honey, that's great! I'm so proud of you. So, does this mean you'll be going to this gala?"

Emma knew exactly the direction her mother was quickly heading. She probably should have had a glass of wine before making the call. "Yes, Mom. I'll be there. But it's a work thing—not a social thing. I'm not bringing a date—no time that night since I'll be *working*. It just wouldn't be fair to my

Tracey L. Ryan

date, now would it?" This should hold her over for a while, Emma thought.

"Maybe you'll meet someone while you are working there. I'm sure there will be plenty of rich hotties there."

"We'll see. But I'm there to work, not find a man."

"What dress are you wearing? Have you gone shopping yet?"

"I was thinking the black strapless gown that I wore to that wedding last year."

"Absolutely not! You must get something new and sassy. Especially if you are going to get the attention of any dashing, single men there. I'm going to pay for it and no arguments!" Why couldn't she have one conversation with her mother that didn't involve her love life, or lack thereof, she thought.

"Mom, I can buy my own dress!"

"No arguments. Consider a congratulations gift." Her mother's happiness seemed to radiate through the phone. It always made Emma feel like her mother hadn't moved across the country.

"Thanks, Mom. How about I go this weekend to Newbury Street to see what I can find? I can text you pictures of any that I like, then you can make the final decision."

"Sounds like a plan, honey." Emma heard the doorbell ring at her mother's house in the background. "Honey, my book club is here. I'll talk to you this weekend. And, honey, I'm so proud of you. Love you."

"Love you too, Mom." Emma hung up the phone and thought, That went well. She knew her mother would press her about the date thing and was thankful for book clubs, otherwise she might not have been able to get off so easy.

CHAPTER 3

———

The rest of Emma's night was quiet and relaxing. As the clock approached nine o'clock, Emma decided to take a shower and go to bed. She turned off the TV and lights, and made her way to the master bedroom suite. In the white marble master bathroom, she turned on the rain shower with the multiple wall-mounted water jets. As she waited for the water to get hot, she realized how tired she was. She stripped down, leaving her clothes crumpled in a pile outside the glass shower. The steam started to slowly escape from the shower stall, filling the oversized bathroom. It was always a place Emma could escape real life and wash away the day's stress. Today was no different.

A wave of steam enveloped her like a cashmere blanket as she stepped inside the shower. She couldn't even see the grey slate tiles that lined two walls of the shower. For the first few minutes, she just let the water flow over her from head to toe. Her thoughts drifted to the gala and then, as her body began to relax, her mind pulled up an image of Hunter. His 6'2" athletic body, his tousled dark hair, and crystal blue eyes washed over her like a wave. His square jaw line that could chisel granite was imprinted on her brain.

She snapped back to reality. Her head and pulse were pounding. Emma quickly washed her hair and body, rinsed, and grabbed the towel from the hook next to the shower. She was still struggling to catch her breath as she dried off and couldn't understand why she'd been thinking of Hunter. She was sure it was because of the gala and knowing she'd be sure to see him. She put the towel back on the hook, ran a brush through her damp hair, and walked in the bedroom naked.

The floor-to-ceiling windows in the bedroom made the city look alive at night. The lights twinkled like the stars watching from above. Emma thought it was magical to lie in bed and watch the city. She knew that anyone with a telescope could probably see her, but she didn't care. She always liked being naked in her bedroom with all the drapes open. She felt a little like an exhibitionist, but it was also so liberating.

The room was decorated in a modern style with a pale lavender color scheme. The king size bed looked out to the ocean, which sometimes created the illusion of being on a Caribbean cruise. Although there were the same cherry hardwoods in here as the rest of the condo, Emma had added a steel grey, plush area rug under the bed, so it wasn't as cold in the winter. The white sheer drapes were always left open so she could see the outside world.

Emma pulled back the lavender and taupe silk comforter with matching sheets and crawled into the dark truffle king size platform bed with the intricately carved headboard. She always loved the feel of cool silk against her soft skin. It felt like she was in a cocoon as the silk draped over every curve of her body. Whenever she moved, the sheets followed every move with precision.

She decided to forego her standard *Criminal Minds* Monday marathon given how drained she felt. Her head barely hit the pillows before her eyes and body gave into the deep sleep she craved. Entering quickly into a deep REM sleep, her mind relaxed and opened itself to her deepest thoughts. Her breathing started to even out as she rolled to her left side.

Emma felt the light caress of strong hands across her shoulders, down her arm, and down to her buttocks. At the same time, soft lips gently kissed her neck, giving her goose bumps as she rolled on to her back. In the shadows, she could make out the sexy features of her guest as she gently ran her hands through his tousled dark hair. The moonlight caught the crystal blue in his eyes as he smiled at her. He whispered something she couldn't quite make out as he strategically moved on top of her.

His fingers caressed her breasts and nipples before his tongue began to tease them. He sucked and nibbled until her nipples are hard, then continued down the path to her Garden of Eden. She instinctively spread her legs, giving him full access as his tongue danced around her most private area, setting her on fire. The teasing seemed to go on for an eternity, igniting every molecule of her body.

The alarm promptly went off at 6:25 a.m. with the sound of KISS 108's *Matty in the Morning*. Emma was startled awake, a bit disoriented. As the sunlight filtered into the room, she looked around to see that she was alone. Her comforter and sheets were thrown to one side of the bed as she lay naked. Her heart pounded as she tried to control her emotions.

As the weather report came on, she stretched and rolled out of bed. She continued her morning ritual of walking to the window to look out at the city as it started to awaken. Her thoughts this morning drifted back to her unusually erotic dream. It's been a long time since she felt something so sensual, in dreamland or reality. Maybe her mother was right, she needed to start dating more. The thought of this made her shutter as she moved to the shower to start her day.

Tracey L. Ryan

CHAPTER 4

___

The rest of the week was busy putting together the final project plans for the gala and finishing up work on a few smaller marketing campaigns for other clients. The team was still on cloud nine, working late, and letting the creative juices flow like a tsunami.

At four o'clock on Friday, Emma told the team to go home and enjoy the weekend. Her instructions were clear - under no circumstances were they to come in over the weekend or bring work home. She needed them fresh and well-rested for Monday. Everyone looked happy, except Evan who started to protest until he saw Emma's expression, which stopped him in mid-sentence.

While the team fled to the elevator like they were trying out for the Boston Marathon, Emma texted her two best friends to confirm dinner tonight and shopping tomorrow. Morgan, Hannah, and Emma had been friends since kindergarten. The rollercoaster of life seemed to keep this trio together over the years. Morgan was a well-respected pediatrician at Boston Children's Hospital, and Hannah was an elementary school teacher at one of Boston's well-known private schools. It was cosmic poetry that all three grew up in Hardwicke and were all living successful lives in Boston. And, as Emma's mother would say, were all very single and available.

They decided to meet at The Stallion Pub at six o'clock on Atlantic Avenue for drinks and dinner. Friday's were usually jam-packed but Morgan was the manager's pediatrician, so they were always able to get a table. With traffic in and out of the city gridlocked every Friday, Emma decided to walk home. It was a beautiful spring day with the sun shining, birds still singing, and mild temperatures for Boston standards. On the way home she could see Hunter's corporate headquarters in the distance. The sun reflected off the rose-hued glass of the tower rising from the concrete creating a giant prism. She really couldn't wait until this whole thing was over so she could return to not thinking of him.

A girls' night out was just what she needed. Next week would be intense with the preparation for the gala plus the interview with the Boston Times. She wondered what she had gotten herself into as she walked up to her building. The building had some of the best security in the city, requiring each tenant to swipe a key card to enter the main doors then enter their specific key code to enter the interior lobby doors. Emma rarely saw a security guard in the traditional sense but knew there was behind-the-scenes security that monitored camera footage 24/7. Even the elevator required a tenant-specific key code since each floor opened directly into the tenant's foyer.

When the elevator doors slid open, Emma punched in her code and the doors silently closed. She was whisked up to her floor in a matter of seconds. After unlocking the foyer door, she went straight to her home office to drop off her Coach briefcase. Her home office afforded her almost the same incredible views as her daytime office did. Emma had really wanted to make sure this space wasn't stuffy or too masculine, yet still had a modern feel. For the wall color, she had chosen a warm, butter yellow. One wall was taken up by a six-piece bookcase and file cabinet unit. The mahogany writing desk with curved cabriole legs had been a gift from her father just before his death. Every time she came into the room, she felt he would be proud of how things had turned out for her.

She kicked off her Jimmy Choo's as she entered the bedroom and found herself glancing at the bed, triggering a flashback of her dream. She shook her head and began to undress. She threw her black checkered Ralph Lauren pant suit and grey silk camisole into the "must dry clean" pile—a pile that was quickly growing to a large mountain and threatening to take over. She chastised herself - if she didn't get to the dry cleaner soon, she not only would have nothing to wear but also wouldn't have any room left on the floor of her closet.

Emma stood in only a black lace demi-bra and matching thong in her custom designed walk-in closet with cedar shelving and slide out shoe drawers. She had no shortage of work clothes to choose from, but always found it hard to dress for the casual nights out. She decided on a hot pink Tommy Hilfiger cotton shirtdress with cap sleeves that fell about six inches above the knee. The Michael Kors black peek-a-boo platforms would go with it perfectly. Since it was girls' night out, simple but dazzling jewelry was a must.

She laid the dress out on the bed, then decided to take a quick shower. She let the water get steamy and hot but knew she had to hurry as she only had forty minutes to get to The Stallion. The rule was that whoever was last to arrive had to buy the first round of drinks. She quickly washed and dried, threw her hair up and applied minimal makeup. Emma stopped by the hall mirror for one last look before bolting out the door in hopes of not being last for once. Luckily, it was only a couple blocks from her place so there was a shimmer of hope.

It was a typical Friday night in Boston. Every restaurant and bar on the waterfront was packed to the gills, some with lines already out the door.

Tracey L. Ryan

Emma rounded the corner to see The Stallion in front of her. She made it with fifteen minutes to spare. Emma squeezed through the entrance and gently pushed her way to the hostess stand where she saw Tricia, the manager, busy seating those waiting. Tricia waved to Emma through the sea of people.

When she finally reached Tricia, Tricia smiled. "Hi, Emma. Bad news—you're last again. Drinks are on you tonight. Sorry, hon!"

"Oh crap! I seriously thought I was going to beat them this time!"

"I'll let Amy show you to your table. Enjoy!"

Amy appeared out of nowhere and told Emma to follow her. They maneuvered through the throngs of people and tables to their usual table next to the window. "Thanks, Amy," Emma said with a smile.

"Enjoy your dinner. I think Ricky is your server tonight." Then Amy hurried back to the front of the restaurant.

"Look who finally decided to grace us with her presence!" Hannah shouted, laughing.

"Yes, your highness, drinks are on you!" Morgan managed to get out before laughing.

"I really thought I had you both beat this time. I swear you girls tell me one time and you plan an earlier time so you can be sure you'll be here before me." Emma pretended to pout before laughing.

"Don't get all paranoid on us. You lost fair and square. Now pay up—we want drinks," Hannah said as she flipped her long brown hair and smiled. "So, what shall we start off with tonight? I need something strong. Those kids are driving me nuts with spring fever. If I get asked how many days left until school is out again, I think I will scream." Hannah let out a little sigh for the appropriate amount of affect.

Just as the trio was looking over the drink menu, Ricky appeared with a chilled bottle of Moet & Chandon champagne and three glasses.

"Hi, Ricky. Um, we didn't order this," Morgan said with a puzzled look on her face.

"Hello, ladies. Apparently one, or all of you, has a secret admirer with extremely good taste. All I was told was to deliver it to this table and tell you that refusal was not an option."

As Ricky finished his speech, for which he had received a very handsome tip, the crowd started to part like Moses and the Red Sea, revealing one of the world's wealthiest and eligible bachelors making his way to the Girls' Night Out table.

Ricky saw him approaching and almost dropped the bottle of champagne. "Mr. Logan, your champagne has been delivered as you requested." Ricky discretely made his exit.

Tracey L. Ryan

CHAPTER 5

I t was the first time in ten years that Emma looked into those piercing blue eyes that seemed to be made of arctic ice and heard his brilliant British acccnt. "Good evening, ladies. A celebration isn't a true event until you enjoy the best champagne. Emma, congratulations on winning the Children's Hospital Gala contract. I look forward to working with you on this very important event." He couldn't seem to keep his eyes off Emma, which unnerved her.

"I don't want to interrupt what looks to be a fun-filled girl's night out. I just wanted to personally congratulate you. Enjoy your evening." As Hunter swaggered back towards the front of the restaurant with his best friend and head of security, Ryan Donavan, all Emma could do was stare.

"Ok, girlfriend, you need to spill right now! What the hell was that all about? I didn't know you were still in contact with him. He was like a dog marking his freaking territory." Morgan was always the first to jump onto juicy gossip.

"Morgan be quiet. I think Emma is about to have a stroke or something. She looks a bit pale."

"Look, I haven't seen or talked to him in ten years. I absolutely have no idea why he just did that. I knew I'd have to see him at the event but…I just…have no idea." Emma reached for her glass of champagne and downed it like she was doing a shot of tequila. Her hands were shaking, and her heart felt like it was about to jump out of her body onto the table.

Both of her friends could see she was visibly shaken. Hannah was the first to respond. "Hey, maybe he just happened to be here, saw you, and thought he'd break the ice knowing he was going to have to see you for all the gala stuff. Let's chalk it up to him being nice and not a prick. Now let's get some real drinks and order dinner. I'm starving."

Hannah always had this unique way to calm any situation, Emma thought. Emma was glad her friends decided to forget the incident and continue with girls' night as planned. All three ordered their usual, which made Ricky chuckle. He knew what they were having as soon as he saw them come into the restaurant and had already told the chef. Hannah always ordered the grilled salmon, Morgan had roasted duck, and Emma was the grilled tenderloin. Typically, the women did not order dessert - they figured they were drinking enough calories. Tonight was different—it was a celebration—so they opted to each get the crème brûlée.

Tracey L. Ryan

As Ricky was clearing their plates, he announced "You ladies are all set. Your bill was paid in full by Mr. Logan. He also said that if you wish to stay here and continue drinking, that would also be taken care of."

Emma stared at Ricky and blinked several times. All she could think was - why was this happening? Why was he suddenly intruding in her life? Both Hannah and Morgan were staring at Emma. Emma finally said, "Ricky, although that was very kind of Mr. Logan, we can pay our own tab."

"No can do, sweets. He was rather insistent, and I don't really want to piss off the boss man."

"Boss? Do you mean Hunter owns this place?"

"Yup. Bought it last year when the last owner was basically running it into the ground. All I heard was he bought it for a song, and it's been thriving ever since. Must be because of his devilish good looks and that damn British accent," Ricky chuckled.

"Is Mr. Logan still here by chance?"

"Um, I can check. I think I still saw his security guy, Ryan, around here not too long ago. And Ryan is never far behind Mr. Logan. I'll be back in a flash." And before any of them could say another word, Ricky was maneuvering through the crowd towards what looked like the offices.

The other two women were still staring at Emma as they noticed Emma's mood turn from shaken to stirred like a martini. She had the fury of a hornet whose nest was just poked with a burning stick and was definitely on her way to quickly blowing a fuse.

"Emma, you need to calm down. Don't do anything stupid. You've had a couple cocktails, so you have booze balls. Like I said before, he is just being nice for once in his life," Hannah said, desperately trying to avoid the scene which was about to erupt.

"Hunter doesn't do anything without a reason. Have you ever known him to do something nice just for the sake of it when we were growing up? He always has an agenda and I will be *damned* if he brings me into it."

"But you haven't seen him for ten years. He may have changed. He lost his dad tragically, too. And you know what effect that can have. Maybe he decided life was too short and he shouldn't waste it being a dumbass," said Hannah, still trying to influence a state of calmness.

Just at that moment, Ricky returned to announce that Mr. Logan was indeed still here in his private office. If Emma wanted to see him, Ricky would be happy to show her the way. Emma popped out of her chair so fast it almost tipped over and told the women she'd be right back. To make sure they didn't strand her there —which they wouldn't normally—she left her purse at the table with them.

Emma seemed to glide across the restaurant with confidence. She didn't even notice how many heads she turned when she walked by. But that was Emma, very unassuming and never taking her natural beauty for granted. She never looked for attention, but attention seemed to follow her.

Ricky knocked on the door to the office, which had a sign saying "Private" on it. The deep British voice on the other side of the door said, "Come in."

Emma's heart skipped a beat and she almost ran back to her table. Before she could, Ricky opened the door and then darted back to his table waiting duties. It was the first time in years that Hunter and Emma were in their own little world. Emma could no longer hear the buzz of the restaurant, even though she technically wasn't even inside the office. It seemed like she was in a time warp as the flood of memories came back to her. Horseback riding at the Logan family's estate in Hardwicke, playing tennis at the country club, watching rugby on television and trying to understand it—it all seemed so innocent and nice.

Within seconds, Hunter had made it across his office to where she stood in the threshold. "Emma, I was hoping you would stop by," he said with the most devilish smile as he ushered her into the office. He closed the door behind them and returned to his desk.

"Look, I wanted to thank you for the champagne but paying for our dinner is not necessary. I insist that we pay for it ourselves." Emma tried to look commanding and in control, although she really wanted to throw up.

"By now you probably know that I own this place. The staff will not accept your money. I won't hesitate to fire anyone who does. It is your choice if you want to be the one responsible for someone being fired." The ruthlessness he was famous for, just like his father, was starting to show.

Emma fired back at him, "Why? We haven't seen each other in ten years. You always have an angle. I just don't know what it is yet."

"Ah, sweet, sweet, Emma. You are very cynical these days. Look, there's no motive or game. I just decided to be nice…for once. But you are starting to make me reassess my grand gesture." Hunter heaved a sigh and stood up from behind his dark, cherry, executive-style desk. As he walked toward Emma, she froze like a marble statue. Her heart was pounding so hard she thought he could see it through her dress.

Hunter gestured for her to sit on the dark brown leather couch that was against the wall closest to the door. "Thanks, but I prefer to stand. I won't be here that long."

"Suit yourself," Hunter said as he slid onto the couch like a cougar watching its prey. "Emma, let's try to be amicable. We have a lot of work to do on this gala, and I don't want any animosity between us. I thought that maybe this gesture tonight would help break the ice, but I see that I may have been wrong." Hunter let that hang in the air for a minute.

It was a business leadership tactic to use silence to your advantage.

Those were virtually the same words that Hannah had used, Emma thought. She wondered if Hunter had their table bugged. "If what you say is true, then I will just say thank you and let you get back to work."

Emma wasn't sure how he was able to get to the office door so quickly, but before she could turn around to leave, he had his hand on the door. Their bodies so close she could feel him breathing. At first, she thought he wasn't going to let her leave and had a momentary panic attack, but he slowly opened the door for her.

"My office will be in touch in the next few weeks to start discussing the details for the event. I think it would be beneficial for you to visit my headquarters so you can get a feel for the layout. Until next time, kitten." The next thing Emma knew was the door closed behind her, and she was once again part of the vibe in the restaurant.

It wasn't until she got back to the table that it hit her, he called her by his pet name for her when they were teenagers. Luckily, her friends knew her better than she knew herself sometimes—they had a watermelon martini waiting for her.

"Okay, you look in one piece. Not sure what he looks like. Clothes aren't disheveled or on backwards, so no quickie in the office." Morgan was always the sarcastic one of the group.

"It was very amicable—to use his word. Hannah, you may have been right. He *said* he just wanted to break the ice—he used your exact words—before we started all the prep work for the gala. His office will call my office in the next few weeks to start nailing down details. He also suggested that I come to his headquarters to get a feel for the space."

"Okay, so what I heard was 'nail' and 'feel'," Morgan said with a smug look on her face. "I think he wants to nail you in his space." Morgan cracked herself up.

Emma rolled her eyes, but with a smile said, "You *are* nuts!"

"Oh, please, like you haven't thought about it! Look at him—even if he is a little ass prick—he's still sexy as hell! What I'd give to find out what that body can do and how long he can do it."

"Then you have a go at him, Morgan. I have a job to do—this is business and definitely *NOT* pleasure!" Emma was more upset at herself than at Morgan, given the direction her own thoughts had taken relating to Hunter.

"And Emma goes home alone again. Em, face it, you *never* got over him. We were both there to see how devastated you were when your father flat out forbade you to have anything to do with him or his family. And when Hunter never came to visit when he was on break, you cried for weeks. And he never saw what it did to you. Plus, he never bothered to write or call you. To hell with him!"

"I hate to remind you, but that was high school, and it was called having a crush on someone. It never would have worked anyhow. We are obviously from two very different planets." Emma tried to pretend that it hadn't hurt when Hunter had just disappeared from her life. She always had a feeling his father had something to do with it, given his reputation for being an overall controlling bastard. She never wanted to think that Hunter just got tired of his summertime friend.

"The more you protest, the more I think you still have a thing for him." Morgan insisted in trying to keep the conversation going on this topic.

"Okay, conversation over, Morgan. If you both would like to move on to the next location, we can, as long as there is no more Hunter Logan talk. This topic is officially off limits." The trio had a pact that if one of them said a particular topic was off limits, the others would respect that and not bring it up again.

"Okay, let's go have one more drink and call it a night. We have a busy day of Newbury Street shopping tomorrow." Hannah always could bring them back to reality. The trio decided on Brady's for their martini nightcap. After Brady's, the women hugged each other, got in their respective cabs, and went home.

Emma couldn't stop thinking about Hunter as

she entered her condo. God, she hoped she didn't dream of him again tonight. She needed to get her mind, and body, to realize that he was a business deal. Nothing more, nothing less. She didn't bother to turn on any extra lights as she was just going to jump in the shower and go to bed. The shower had its usual relaxing effect on her. It was 1 a.m. by the time she crawled under the cool silk sheets. She needed to get some sleep—shopping with those two was an exhausting day in the making.

CHAPTER 6

———

S he woke up to her alarm at 8 a.m., completely rested and dream-free. As she stretched, she realized how draining the day would be. Morgan and Hannah had very different styles than Emma's, which would make this more of a challenge. And after last night's escapades—both were sure to be trying to find the skimpiest, sexiest dress they could for Emma.

It was a bit cloudy and cool, so Emma chose to wear casual black slacks with a V-neck light pink cashmere sweater. They would undoubtedly be doing a fair amount of walking, so her Bandalino two-inch chunk heel shoes would do the trick. One last look in the hallway mirror, and Emma was out the door to meet her friends at Luce's Boutique.

Two hours into this shopping adventure, and with nothing to show for it, they decided to try LeMilan. Morgan convinced them that they would have formal gowns and probably the largest selection. Unbeknownst to Emma and Hannah,

Morgan had made an appointment with the owner already. When they arrived, they were greeted with champagne and approximately fifteen dresses for Emma to try on ranging in different colors, lengths, and styles.

Finally, after another two hours, they narrowed down the choices to a Gemy strapless full-length silk gown in black or a Georges Chakra single shoulder strap high-front slit full-length gown in pale pink. The store owner, Hannah, and Morgan all agreed that the Georges Chakra was the one. Emma thought that she could've just stayed home and let all of them shop for her. Now that that decision was made, next was to take a picture and text her mother.

Within minutes, her cell phone was ringing. "Hi, Mom."

"Honey, that dress is absolutely stunning. You will definitely have your choice of dance partners that night. Please put the store clerk on so I can give them my credit card info."

Emma handed the phone to the owner who took down the information and rang up the sale. Luckily, Emma was a perfect size 6 so no alterations were needed. The owner had just ordered one for a wedding party, but the wedding ended up being canceled so she had it there in the store for Emma to take home with her.

As it was past lunch time, the trio decided to get

some quick appetizers on Newbury Street before going their separate ways for the rest of the day. All in all, the day wasn't as grueling as Emma had thought it would be. Unlike some women, she never really enjoyed shopping. Most of the time it aggravated her, but today had been a good day. A good weekend in fact.

The rest of the weekend was the mundane routine of cleaning her condo, grocery shopping, and other various errands. Sunday night came fast and furious as she settled in on the couch to watch *Independence Day* for the 100th time and began to drift off. Emma decided that at 10 p.m. it was time for a shower and then bed. Her nightly ritual seldom changed—dinner in front of the TV in the living room, 30-minute hot shower, then crawling into bed.

The shower totally wiped her out and she decided to not turn on the TV in the bedroom. Her skinned tingled when it felt the coolness of the sheets after the hot shower. The mattress formed around her body as the sheets softly fell upon her skin. Her eyes closed as she got comfortable on her left side and drifted off to parts unknown.

The same dream of Hunter crept into her mind and was a continuation of the last one. His tongue sadistically teased her Garden of Eden. She started to whimper as her entire body tingled with every touch. His tongue continued to lick and suck as he slowly used his strong fingers to explore. He started circling and teasing, feeling her wetness. He smiled with pleasure and satisfaction as he knew that he was responsible for her being completely under his spell. He made a show of licking his two fingers and in one quick motion, thrust them deep into her so that her body convulsed with pleasure. She arched her back in response to his exploration of her deepest secrets and lets out a scream.

The alarm clock once again promptly went off at 6:25 a.m. to *Matty in the Morning* on KISS 108. Emma was startled awake, damp with sweat. Once again, the comforter and sheets were thrown to one side of the bed, so her nakedness was there for the world to see. Her whole body tingled as she sat up in bed. Her mind was spinning as she headed to the shower. She needed a clear head for this week—there was too much going on. As she lathered soap all over her body in the shower, her hand briefly stopped on the location from the porn movie she had in her dream. She quickly dismissed the thoughts, rinsed and stepped out of the shower.

CHAPTER 7

T he rest of that Monday was uneventful for Emma. The staff was all busy on their To-Do's for the project. The interview with the Boston Times was scheduled for the coming Wednesday. Things were semi-normal for her, at least at the office. The private line in her office started ringing as she was preparing for the upcoming newspaper interview. She silently reminded herself to do some research on the reporter so she wouldn't be caught off-guard.

"Emma, you won't guess who is calling for you!" Ashley screamed into the phone. Emma thought, here we go again.

"I am going to guess it is Hunter Logan," Emma blurted out without thinking.

"How did you know? That takes the surprise out of it," Ashley said, slightly defeated. Before Emma could say anything else, Ashley transferred the call to Emma's office.

"Hello, Emma. I trust that you are having a

nice Monday." Even his voice was sexy in a smooth and sophisticated way with an unmistakable British accent. It was confident and authoritative, which Emma found to be a complete turn on.

"I hadn't expected to hear from you so quickly. I thought you would have one of your minions call for anything to do with the gala."

"Emma, dear, you know me so little. I don't staff out the important tasks. I like to take on these challenges myself."

"So, the gala is a challenge to you? I thought it was a worthy charity event?"

"Not the gala, my dear." Emma's world was spinning. Why was he doing this to her? "I was wondering if you would be free for lunch tomorrow so that I may show you the space for the event."

Emma paused briefly—was he asking her to lunch or was this just a task to check-off his To-Do list? "Tomorrow at 11:30 would work for me if you are available. If you are not available, I can either do it another day or you can have someone on your staff show me the space."

"I will make sure that I am available to person-ally give you the full tour. Tomorrow at 11:30 it is then. Good day." Hunter hung up before Emma could respond. Once again, Emma was left not sure whether she was reading too much into the conversation or not enough as she sat there staring at the phone.

The rest of the day was spent with countless meetings, meetings to prep for meetings, and conference calls about meetings. Emma thoroughly enjoyed owning her own business, seeing how far the business had come, knowing it was because of her it existed in the first place—it was the countless meetings she had a hard time with. She never felt that meetings to prep for meetings were beneficial or worthwhile, but it was part of the business, so she learned to adjust.

Ashley was still star-struck at the end of the day that she got to speak with Mr. Logan, as she kept insisting on calling him all day. "Mr. Logan this," and "Mr. Logan that." Emma was exhausted hearing that name for eight straight hours.

It was nearing five o'clock when Ashley poked her head into Emma's office. "Emma, okay if I leave a few minutes early? I have a date tonight and want to make sure I'm ready when he picks me up."

Emma arched her brow. "A date? Is this a new one or an old flame?"

"A new one. His name is Greg and I met him on one of those online dating sites. We're going to dinner and a movie. How retro, huh?" Ashley giggled like she was in junior high.

"I don't think it's retro; it sounds very nice. Well, have a great time. I'll see you in the morning."

"Ciao for now! Oh - don't forget you have that lunch date with Mr. Logan tomorrow. I would suggest you wear something uber-sexy to drive him crazy." With that, Ashley flew out the door and onto the elevator, not giving Emma the chance to respond.

Emma sighed. She really couldn't wait for all of this to be over with. She had a pang of jealousy—even Ashley was dating. All she kept hoping was that she didn't end up like Evan: alone with two cats. With that thought, she shut down her tablet, grabbed her briefcase, and locked her office.

The short elevator ride down to the lobby didn't offer Emma much relief from thoughts of Hunter. She was thinking about what the elevators in his lobby must be like compared to this one when the doors slid open. Ryan stood in front of her.

"Good evening, Emma." Ryan was also tall, dark, and handsome, although most would say not as handsome as Hunter. He had a commanding physical presence; one you could only get by working out rigorously every day. Emma noticed some grey hairs, even though Ryan shaved his head every other day.

"Ryan, to what do I owe this unexpected pleasure?" Emma smiled almost flirtatiously.

"I tried calling your office, but it just went to voicemail. So, I thought I'd see if I could catch you before you left."

"Well, you caught me. What can I do for you?"

"Hunter asked me to pick you up tomorrow for your lunch meeting. I wanted to let you know that I would be here at 11:15 in the midnight blue Mercedes that's parked outside the building now."

As they walked to the front doors of the lobby, Emma caught a glimpse of the new Mercedes-Benz S550 4Matic sedan. The car was almost as stunning as Hunter himself, she thought. Ryan could see Emma admiring the car from the corner of his eye and smiled slyly, hoping she didn't see.

"Ryan, although I appreciate Hunter's offer for a ride, I can either drive myself or take a cab. It's no bother."

"Unfortunately, I was told not to take 'no' for an answer. I will see you at 11:15 tomorrow morning. If you want my advice, *off the record*, be careful, Emma. This charity thing is a great cause and all, but I'm not sure what else he's looking for with all of this. I know you two go way back. I don't know what exactly happened, nor do I want to. Just watch out for yourself. He's been unsettled since his father died and doesn't always care about the carnage he leaves behind."

"Why are you telling me this? Doesn't this go against some sort of code of ethics or something?" Emma's head started to hurt.

"Look, all I'm saying is don't expect anything from him and you will be fine. Can I offer you a lift home while I am here?"

"Thanks, but I have a few errands to run on my walk home. I appreciate the offer, though. I'll see you tomorrow." Emma lied about the errands as she didn't want to have this conversation continue.

"See you tomorrow, Ms. Sharpeton." Ryan turned off the car alarm and hopped in the driver's seat. Within seconds he was speeding down the street weaving in and around other cars like they were standing still.

CHAPTER 8

———

Emma kept replaying the conversation in her mind as she walked home, so distracted she almost walked past her building. Once inside her condo, she tried to restore some normalcy to her day by getting into her typical after-work routine. Tonight, she decided on pasta with marinara sauce. When her pasta was cooked and on the plate, she padded to the living room to watch TV. She opted for a movie tonight instead of the typical *Criminal Minds*-type shows. She settled on *Growing Defiant,* a feel-good movie where everyone got their happy ending.

After dinner and the movie, Emma still wasn't relaxed or all that tired. She was a little nervous to go to sleep at all given her recent crazy dreams. Plus, she knew she had the meeting with Hunter tomorrow. What does "uber-sexy" mean anyhow? she wondered.

The shower did the trick, relaxing every muscle in Emma's body. She honestly felt like she had just had a massage. She put the towel back on the hook and walked into her closet. She sighed as she took inventory of her clothes—nothing rang out "uber-sexy." She settled on the Ralph Lauren cap-sleeved quinlan dress in taupe with matching 3-inch strappy sandals. Although the hemline fell just above her knees, the wrap-around style in the front would provide some scenery for Mr. Logan when she crossed her legs, Emma thought.

Now that that was settled, Emma crawled into bed, turned the TV on to help her fall asleep, and wriggled around until she found a comfy spot. The alarm went off at the normal time, and Emma stretched and yawned. She got a very undisturbed seven hours of sleep and felt refreshed for a change.

The trek into work was business as usual until Emma stepped out of the elevator into her office space, and Ashley practically jumped over the reception desk to greet her. Obviously, her date had gone well last night was all Emma could think.

"Morning, Ashley. I take it you had a good time last night."

Ashley followed Emma into her office. As Emma unpacked her briefcase and got settled in, Ashley proceeded to tell her about her "enchanting evening with Mr. Right." At least Ashley knew enough to get Emma's English Breakfast tea before letting the deluge of details spew out.

"Oh, Emma, he's the one! He's gorgeous, sexy, wicked smart, and just makes my body go all tingly."

Emma tried to act interested but knew that the inevitable details were only moments away. She smiled at Ashley as the sooner this was over, the better for both of them.

"The dinner and movie were fun, but it was afterward that was…I don't know how to say it. He rocked my world, Em! I mean screaming, head banging against the headboard, rocking my world. For hours. I'm surprised I can even function today. The things he did, well, I didn't know they were even possible." At that moment, Emma's phone rang, and she said a silent prayer of gratitude.

"Emma Sharpeton."

"Good morning, Miss Emma. I am just confirming our lunch date for 11:30." Emma didn't know which was worse: TMI from Ashley or the "uber-sexy" British voice on the other end of the phone.

"Good morning, Hunter." Ashley's eyes went wide, and she quickly sprinted out of the office and closed the door. "Yes, we are still on for 11:30. Ryan stopped by yesterday to inform me that I would have an escort to your office today."

"I hope you don't mind. I just thought it might be a little easier."

"It was thoughtful of you. My nine o'clock appointment is here. I will see you later." Emma hung up. There was no nine o'clock appointment—

she just couldn't take all this drama in the first fifteen minutes of work.

The morning seemed to fly by, which Emma was thankful for. At 11:10 a.m., Ashley promptly escorted Emma from her impromptu hallway meeting with the design team to her office to collect her bag and get her downstairs for 11:15 a.m. The whole office was whispering about Emma's date, which was driving her insane. She wanted to scream at the top of her lungs, "*THIS IS NOT A DATE— IT'S BUSINESS!*" But she refrained, smiled, and let out a sigh as the elevator doors shut behind her. For a few minutes she would have complete solitude except for the classical music playing on the elevator speakers.

When the doors gracefully slid open, Ryan stood waiting for her, smiling. "Good morning, Emma. Are you ready to go to the Ares Logan Industries headquarters?"

"As ready as I'll ever be, I guess."

Ryan put his hand on the small of Emma's back and gently guided her to the same parked Mercedes she had seen the previous evening.

As Ryan opened the passenger door for Emma, he couldn't help but notice how beautiful she was. He only hoped that Hunter wouldn't be the complete ass he typically was. As Ryan walked around back of the car, he shook his head. Lately, Hunter tended to be very reckless.

Ryan and Hunter had been college roommates for all four years. They had similar backgrounds— both were of Irish and English descent, both of their fathers were ruthless businessmen, and both men were *the* definition of one-night stands. After Hunter's father died a few years ago in a suspicious plane crash in the Amazon, Hunter had taken over Ares Logan Industries, which was a conglomerate of media, pharmaceutical manufacturing, biotechnology, and consulting that his father had started. Ryan had taken a different path after college and had been recruited by the CIA. The men had never spoken of what Ryan had done for the CIA, but Hunter had known that when the time was right, Ryan was the perfect choice for his head of security. Ryan had started working for Hunter a year ago and hadn't looked back.

Boston traffic was light at this time of day on a Tuesday, so they were able to get to Hunter's headquarters within fourteen minutes. Ryan pulled to the curb at the front of the building and quickly jumped out to open the door for Emma. As Ryan offered his hand to help Emma out of the car, all she could do was stare up into the clouds at the magnificent skyscraper in front of her. It was always beautiful from a distance; up close it was breath-taking.

"It does kind of take your breath away, doesn't it?"

Emma could only nod at Ryan's comment. He once again needed to nudge Emma forward and into the front lobby. Emma's eyes got wide as she tried to take in the architectural design and overall splendor of what she was seeing. When Hunter stepped into her view, she almost stumbled back into Ryan.

"I hope you're pleased with what you've seen so far." Hunter let his cunning smile linger until he was sure that Emma has seen it before he continued. "If you would give me one minute. I need to discuss something with Ryan. Please feel free to walk around to get a feel for the space."

Emma did as she was told, wondering if they were talking about her. She quietly scolded herself for even thinking that. As she was looking at the amazing courtyard park with real trees, plants and grass, she could feel Hunter looking at her. She could smell his Versace Pour Homme cologne and feel his breath on her neck.

"This is very beautiful, Hunter. I *am* impressed."

"I'm glad you like it. I thought that we might have lunch first in my office and then do a tour."

Without another word he gently took her by the elbow to lead her to his private elevator, which he needed both a key code and swipe card to open the doors and request a floor. They were whisked up to the thirtieth floor in an all glass elevator that looked at the interior of the building on one side and the harbor on the other side. Emma felt like a kid at an amusement park. Hunter watched Emma's expressions as they rode up to his office. He was both amused and mystified by this woman he had not seen in years.

The doors opened directly into Hunter's private office. Like Emma's building, there were floor-to-ceiling windows throughout the space. His office was the entire top floor of the building and decorated with a sophisticated, masculine style with plenty of dark wood, leather, and muted colors. Although there were few walls, the space was clearly divided. A large mahogany executive desk with matching credenzas and bookshelves were one corner of the space. On the opposite corner was a dark brown leather sofa, two matching leather wingback chairs, with coordinating cherry coffee table and end tables. On the floor in that corner was a cream-colored plush area rug.

As Emma was taking in the office, Hunter whispered, "Please make yourself comfortable on the sofa. I will go make us some drinks." Emma watched him swagger to the built-in bar on the opposite wall. There was a full refrigerator, sink, mini-wine cellar plus any top-shelf liquor you could think of. He opened the fridge to pull out a perfectly chilled bottle of Holloran Oregon Rose´ and opened it gracefully, showing Emma he had practice doing this.

Hunter returned to the sofa with two glasses of the expensive wine and offered a toast, "To raising the bar for the gala. Salute." He gently tapped Emma's glass as she managed to return his toast with, "To the gala. Salute."

Both took a sip of the crisp, pale pink wine and smiled at its robust yet delicate flavor. Emma was a bit uncomfortable partly because of the dress she was wearing and partly because Hunter was sitting only inches away. The phone on the desk buzzed, and Emma let out a little sigh of relief. She wasn't sure how she was going to make it through lunch. Hunter strode over to his desk and pushed the speaker button. "Yes?"

"Sorry to disturb you, sir. I wanted to inform you that your lunch is on its way up." Before Hunter could walk back to the sofa, the elevator doors opened and the aromatic smells of the meal began to permeate the office. A man, who Emma could only surmise was the chef due to his uniform and puffy hat, wheeled in a large cart filled with covered dishes. Behind the chef was an assistant who went directly to the conference table that was on the same side of the office as the desk, laid out a white crisp linen tablecloth, silverware, and Lenox china. Once the table was setup, the chef removed the covers of the chaffing pans and prepared the food for presentation on the plates.

"I wasn't sure what you liked for lunch, so I

ordered a medley. If you don't like anything here, the chef will make you something more to your liking."

"I'm sure this will be great. It smells wonderful." Emma smiled at the chef and assistant, hoping they understood her gratitude for their hard work. She would eat whatever was there as she didn't want to get either of them in trouble with their boss.

Emma tried, as gracefully as she could, to get up from the sofa and walk over to the table. On the plates were Caesar salad, thinly sliced tenderloin beef, asparagus with béarnaise sauce, and red roasted potatoes. She let out a sigh of relief as this was something she could eat and enjoy, all but the asparagus and hopefully the sauce would drown out the actual taste.

Hunter slid up behind Emma. She once again smelled his cologne and felt his breath on her neck. He reached around one side of her to pull out the chair for her and when she was seated, he gently placed the white linen napkin in her lap. Emma had to keep reminding herself that this was a business lunch, nothing more. Although she never knew the real reason her father had forbidden her from getting involved with Hunter, she trusted her father and knew he must have had a good reason. There was that little voice in her head now, reminding her of that.

"This looks delicious. I can't believe you have your own chef."

Hunter sat at his end of the conference table and smiled at Emma as he dug into his lunch. Emma took that as her queue to start eating. Neither said much during the meal, which was a bit awkward. Once again, the buzzer on the desk phone went off. "Excuse the interruption, the chef is bringing up dessert momentarily."

This time, Hunter didn't respond to the woman on the other end. The elevator doors slid open and the same chef and assistant wheeled in a smaller cart with crème brûlée and an assortment of teas. The assistant began to clear the table as quickly and quietly as possible. Once the lunch dishes were cleared, the chef presented both Emma and Hunter with their dish of freshly made crème brûlée. The chef and assistant then disappeared almost as swiftly as they had appeared.

"I noticed that you ordered this for dessert at the restaurant the other night, so I thought that we could have it today as well," Hunter remarked with a grin.

Emma just blinked at Hunter. He was watching what she ate that night? "Thanks. That was nice of you to go to the trouble. I do love crème brûlée." She couldn't think of anything else to say.

Crème brûlée always seemed to have a sexual connotation to Emma - the rich, creaminess with the hard-melted sugar on top. She could feel herself starting to blush when she noticed Hunter staring at her.

"Shall we finish our wine then go on our tour?" Nothing seemed to faze him, which drove Emma crazy. Although she couldn't quite explain why. "Sure," was all she could say.

Hunter took her hand and led her back to the sofa where their wine was waiting for them. As Emma cautiously sat down, careful not to accidentally flash Hunter, she once again took in his features. He was obviously older now, but he had improved with age, she thought.

"So, I'm sure that your staff is busy with all the preparations for the gala. Care to give me a hint as to how things are going?" There was that devilish grin again.

"Things are progressing nicely. This was a large task—not only did we need to do the marketing campaign, but also plan the actual event, which is slightly different from what we're used to. It's a real honor for my team, though. All of the project planning is complete, now it's on to the fun stuff." Emma always beamed when she talked about her work and her team, and Hunter could see how proud she was of both. Hunter had been following Emma's career for years from afar and found it oddly refreshing to be talking about it in person.

"Sounds like you have made some good progress. I look forward to seeing your design mockups when they are ready. And if you need anything from my staff, please let me know. I will personally see to it you have everything you need," Hunter commented before taking one last swig of his now room temperature wine.

Just as Emma finished her glass, Hunter's hand was out to help her off the sofa. It felt strange to be touching him, but Emma was glad that the touch wasn't sending shockwaves through her body. Maybe it was just in her head after all.

CHAPTER 9

They walked to the elevator, which seemed to automatically sense Hunter approaching and opened its doors. Hunter pressed the Lobby button, and they were off. Going down was a bit more hair-raising than going up, Emma realized. Being in all glass, including the floor, it felt like she was falling off the building, which almost made Emma queasy. Hunter could see Emma getting a bit wobbly and held her elbow to steady her.

"You get used to it after a while. Try not to look down—look out at the ocean. It's a rather calm day on the water." Emma hated to admit it, but Hunter was right: looking out at the deep blue ocean on the horizon helped steady her during this amusement park ride he called an elevator. The sun glistened off the water like millions of diamonds creating as sense of tranquility.

As the elevator slowly came to a stop, Hunter held the doors open so that Emma could step out onto the marble floor of the lobby. She thought about kissing the ground but figured that was a bit over the top, and she knew she wouldn't be able to do it gracefully in her dress.

Hunter started their tour with why he chose that particular architect, how he had a hand in the design, how the building was certified green, and so on. Emma felt like taking a nap after the large lunch, wine, and Hunter's droning on. The design of the lobby was miraculous and breathtaking. You truly felt like you were outside instead of inside one of Boston's largest skyscrapers. The park would be perfect for the gala with warm, white twinkle lights on the trees and a string quartet playing softly in the background as guests arrived. They would need to build a small stage for the live entertainment and lay down a dance floor. Anyone trying to dance on this marble is sure to kill themselves. The possibilities for this space were endless, Emma imagined.

"I get the distinct feeling you aren't listening to a word I've said." They abruptly stopped. Hunter stood directly in front of Emma, towering over her like the trees in the indoor park.

"Sorry. That was rude of me. It's just that this space is perfect. I have so many ideas going through my head I think I just gave myself a headache." She chuckled.

"I can see the creative juices flowing. That is one of the many things that makes you fascinating, you can take a basic space like this and visualize something grand. It's a talent you should be proud of."

Is he complimenting me? Emma wondered "Thanks. I hope I can live up to the expectations. Oh my God! Is it really two o'clock?" She noticed the time on Hunter's TAG Heuer Carrera Calibre watch.

"Afraid it is. Let me guess, you need to be going." Hunter was surprised that he was mildly disappointed.

"I'm so sorry. Thank you for lunch and the tour. If I have questions, I will call you. I may need to come back to get exact dimensions for the space." Emma couldn't believe she said that she might have to come back—that was something she always had her staff do.

"You are most welcome. Feel free to return any time you wish. I am happy to help you in any way I can. Until next time." Hunter reached down and kissed her hand and did the kind of gentlemanly curtsies only seen in movies.

From out of nowhere, Ryan appeared at Emma's side, almost startling her.

"That took a little longer than I expected. Are you ready to go back to your office?"

"Ah, yes, if it's no trouble. If you are busy, I can take a cab, really."

"No can do. The boss said I am to personally escort you back to your office to ensure you arrive safe and sound. Your chariot awaits, my lady." Ryan smiled at Emma as he held the door open for her. Hunter glared at Ryan, but Ryan quietly snickered.

Out on the street, all the serenity of the office vanished. Horns honked, people talked, the endless road construction all snapped Emma back to her reality. Once again, Ryan held the door open for her as she slid into the passenger seat of the Mercedes. And once again, he was like a speeding bullet driving through the mid-afternoon traffic.

Ryan waited for Emma to go into her office building before racing off. Emma watched the car head back to Ares Logan Industries. She stood in her building's lobby for a few minutes trying to make sense of the day's events. What Emma finally decided was that Hunter was trying to see if he could shake her up, had failed miserably, and decided to play nice until this thing was all over. That was her story and she was sticking to it, at least for now.

Emma decided it was time she did her own research on Hunter Logan and his inherited conglomerate. She had heard rumors about his father being a ruthless businessman, and even some that pointed to him being above the law in his mind. Philip Logan was a force to be reckoned with and always seemed to get what he wanted, at any cost. Emma had experienced this a little herself. Was Hunter like his father, and if so, how much?

Tracey L. Ryan

Back at her office, Emma pulled up some interesting internet research on both Hunter and his father. She asked Ashley to make sure she was not disturbed for the rest of the day. The staff was busy working on the materials for the upcoming gala, so no one would wonder what she was doing sequestered in her office. Emma started her investigation with Hunter's father, a man who had scared her by the way he used to look at her. She had known from the first time she met Hunter's father that he had absolutely no use for her. Emma was not in their class, and Philip never tried to hide it. This man had the compassion of a mosquito and the fierceness of a great white shark. It was certainly a strange family dynamic—Hunter's mother was the essence of class and politeness. Emma saw a lot of Hunter's mother in him when they were younger—he was full of life and laughter with a twinkle in his eyes that brought a smile to your face just looking at him.

There were countless articles about Philip Logan. Many were of his business conquests; some were about charity events and a few were about his family. The few family pictures that came up were mostly local charity events that Hunter's mother was the chairperson for. Katherine Logan always looked stunning in her gowns and tasteful jewels. Philip looked as if he wanted to be anywhere but where they were with eyes shooting daggers at the photographer.

As Emma scrolled through the search results, she came across an article with pictures of a Boston Children's Hospital charity event from three years ago. Another posed family picture, probably the last one before Philip had been killed in the plane accident over the Amazon. The strange thing about this photo was that he was smiling, not seething like in every other public picture which intrigued Emma.

Several articles were published around the strange disappearance and presumed death of Philip in South America. Apparently, Hunter's father was an adventurer who enjoyed rock climbing, helicopter skiing, jungle safaris, and so on. The story was that he had gone to South America to try to find clues about a native tribe that vanished back in the 1800s. It was thought that Philip was doing an air survey of the suspected location of the tribe when he ran into engine trouble. Search crews worked for weeks with high tech equipment, air patrols, and foot patrols to try to find him, but eventually the search had been called off. They found the plane wreckage but nothing of its passenger and pilot.

Emma had never really known the story of what happened. At that point in her life, she didn't really care. She had gotten over Hunter and moved on from her humiliation of falling for a boy she obviously couldn't have. A chill ran up her spine just thinking of the last time she saw his father. Hunter had unexpectedly and without a word returned to his English boarding school, literally in the middle of the night. Emma had waited patiently to hear from him, but no letter or phone call ever came. After four days, she had decided to go to his house in hopes that his mother could provide at least an address. Unfortunately, it was Philip who came to the door. Emma almost ran off the front steps as soon as she saw him but decided to hold her ground. He had laughed at her before screaming, "Trash pickup is on Tuesday. My son will never be with anyone who should be picked up with the rest of the trash. Unless you want to make some money— I could use a whore like you when I'm in town." He laughed and then pushed her off the steps. She had fallen backwards down the three steps as Philip slammed the door shut.

Emma tried to push the memory far from her mind and keep reading. All these years and that man still caused her to shiver. It was like he was reaching out from beyond the grave one more time. She kept scrolling through the articles until one caught her eye. The article was about Philip's pharmaceutical company's research on cancer-fighting drugs. The article was a mix of Wall Street mumbo-jumbo and personal history. Apparently, Philip Logan had lost his baby sister to a rare form of cancer when he was twelve years old. He was ten years older than his sister and had been the doting big brother little girls adore. During the interview, Philip said that for the first time in his young life he had felt utterly powerless. Even with all his family's money, there had been nothing they could do to save her. This was his life's mission—to find a pharmaceutical cure in memory of his sister.

For the first time in her life, Emma felt compassion towards this man. An event like that would affect a person and ultimately help shape them into who they became. The article said that Philip threw himself into work at his father's company and basically closed himself off from the rest of the world until his met his wife. That was the first time he seemed to have found happiness since his sister had passed away.

The rest of the articles were focused on his hostile takeovers and building his empire. At the time of his death, he was on the Forbes list of top one hundred wealthiest people with assets estimated at $4.7 billion. Apparently, Hunter inherited the entire company. Katherine was given claims to various houses in the U.S. and Europe plus a very generous lump sum payment but was not allowed anywhere near the family business. Even in death the man was a pompous sexist ass, Emma thought.

Hunter was frequently featured on the local entertainment pages. As he was dubbed the city's most eligible bachelor, it wasn't surprising that every photo also featured him with some gorgeous arm candy. Emma found herself almost seething when she saw the multitude of pictures, all with different women. She was mad at herself for letting her mind wander into the "what if" territory, even if it was in her dreams. Emma smirked as she thought about how she was the one woman Hunter Logan would never have. Money can't buy everything, Emma thought. It was ironic, considering his father had thought she was only after Hunter's money.

The rest of the articles were basically the same—women and money. One thing was certain; Hunter's mission in life besides being a player was to outdo his father in business. Hunter was on last year's Forbes list with an estimated net worth of $6.3 billion. Emma almost fell out of her chair when she read that and sat staring at the screen for the next several minutes. She knew he was beyond rich but had never realized just how much. But money can't buy happiness and it looked like Hunter had a rather lonely existence in her opinion. Then again, she thought, it wasn't like she was going home to a husband and family, so she probably wasn't one to comment.

A gentle knock at the door brought Emma back to reality. Ashley poked her head in to let her know that she was leaving for the night and most of the rest of the staff had already left. Emma said goodnight and got up to stretch. She had been hunched over her tablet for several hours without so much as a break. Her eyes burned from staring at the screen for so long. She decided it was time to head home—she could always pick this back up tomorrow.

As Emma stepped off the elevator in the lobby of her building, she saw Hunter standing next to his polished Mercedes in front of the building. He was chatting with the security guard, who was outside having a cigarette.

The security guard caught sight of Emma and opened the door for her, "Ms. Sharpeton. I hope you had a good day at work today."

"It was an interesting day and looks to be continuing that way."

The security guard decided to make a discreet exit back into the building.

"Hunter, I didn't expect to see you again today."

"Well, you could say that I thrive on spontaneity." Hunter flashed his brightest smile as he nonchalantly started ushering her to his car.

"Where are you taking me, Hunter? And why would I want to go there with you?"

"Ah, always the feisty one. Just relax, it's nothing sinister. Just dinner."

"And why am I having dinner with you?" Emma tilted her head to the side.

"Emma, sometimes you just need to relax and go with the flow." Hunter looked directly into Emma's eyes.

"One of my life's goals isn't to end up on Page Six with you, unlike all the others you trek around the city with," Emma responded with a hint of sarcasm.

"Looks like someone has been doing some exploring. Hmmmm," Hunter said with a satisfied smile. A warm sensation started to overtake Hunter's body at the thought that Emma took the time to dig into his life. Hunter opened the passenger door for her and nudged her into the car before closing the door.

"I don't recall agreeing to go to dinner with you. Look, if you feel the need to drive me somewhere, you can just take me home," Emma replied stubbornly.

Hunter's eyes sparkled and he smirked. "A girl after my own heart: going straight for dessert and skipping dinner."

"That's *NOT* what I meant! Oh God, just drive wherever. You are giving me a migraine." Emma shook her head in annoyance. This was all too much for one day.

Hunter merged into traffic with a smug smile on his face. Out of the corner of his eye he studied this woman who at one time held his heart in her hand. He was convinced back then that they were soul mates, the only person in the world who didn't care about money, just him. Then she shattered his heart when she never returned a single letter he had written from boarding school. His father had warned him that she was only after the money and convinced him that this was for the best. From that point on, Hunter vowed to always protect himself and not look back. One-night stands were easy, there was little chance of being hurt. Both parties got what they wanted out of the deal and there were no complications, as long as he was upfront in the beginning.

The city lights flashed by as Emma gazed silently out the window. She knew the direction they were headed—to the Stallion. How unoriginal, she thought and rolled her eyes. But then again this wasn't a date. She wasn't sure what it was exactly; something dangerous for both of them. They were playing with fire and neither realized how badly they could get burned. Both had been hurt by the other and were now circling like two angry lions, waiting to see which one struck first.

Hunter pulled into his private parking spot and quickly got out to open Emma's door. His put his hand instinctively on the small of her back to guide her into the back entrance. To Emma's surprise the restaurant was closed. Hunter could see the question in her eyes. "I closed the place so that we could have privacy tonight. Probably not the smartest business decision on my part," he said with a devious grin. Emma didn't know how to respond as they walked to the front of the restaurant where a table for two was setup and waiting for them.

Tracey L. Ryan

Hunter pulled out Emma's chair for her and then draped her napkin on her lap. Emma was definitely out of her element and was starting to panic. What game was he playing? Why was she here? Her spidey-sense was in hyper-drive as Hunter bent down and whispered in her ear, "Emma, just breathe and relax. You will soon know why you are here. In the meantime, try to enjoy being with me." Hunter's cologne lingered in the air while me made his way to his own seat across from Emma.

A waiter Emma had never seen before brought calamari and a bottle of Holloran Pinot Noir Glasses were filled and both started eating in silence. Salads came with her favorite dressing, then her favorite entrée was placed in front of her. Emma didn't dare look at Hunter for fear he'd see the panic in her emerald eyes. How could she relax? She was trapped having dinner with him. She knew how ridiculous that sounded as half the women in the city and beyond would die to be sitting where she was.

Before dessert came, Hunter asked the waiter not to disturb them until he signaled that they were ready. When Emma looked up, Hunter was staring at her with heavy eyes. For the first time during this charade he seemed a bit nervous.

"The reason I asked you here tonight is I need to know something before we continue any further with the gala."

A wave of relief came over her. This was about the gala and not them specifically. "What is it? Did you think of something after I left?" Emma's tone transformed to business.

"It's not about the gala details specifically."

Panic rose again through her body like an electric shock causing her pulse to quicken. Her breathing became shallow as she unknowingly sat up straighter.

"I am not one to live in the past, but I find myself not being able to move forward since you literally walked back into my life." Hunter stared at Emma across the table with his intense arctic blue eyes.

"I don't understand." Panic morphed into confusion as her mind raced.

"This event is very important to me…I need to know that you won't walk out on this event like you did with me years ago." He had finally said it out loud. He breathed a little sigh of relief. Hunter was not used to allowing anyone to know his true feelings, but this had been eating him up inside.

Emma stammered, "Wha…what are you talking about?" Then rage started to boil over in her like a wild uncontrollable beast. All the hurt from years past came back with a vengeance. "I walked out on you? Are you fucking insane? YOU are the one who left in the middle of the night without so much as a warning. YOU were the one who never once tried to contact me. When I had the stupid idea of asking how to contact you, your father absolutely humiliated me. And now YOU accuse me of planning to walk out on this event? You are a pompous ass just like your father!" Emma was on a roll and couldn't stop even if she tried. All Hunter could do was stare in disbelief.

She planted both hands squarely on the table as she rose from her chair to meet him eye to eye. "I spent months wondering why you would just leave, and why your father felt the need to not only humiliate me but also to physically push me off the front steps. Then I realized that I was just a joke to you and your demented family. I may not be a billionaire like you, but I have one thing you don't—integrity. I will do my duty with this event and the best job I possibly can."

Hunter stared at the ferocious woman in front of him, barely breathing as her words slowly seeped into his brain.

Emma didn't pause to take a breath. "You are quite a piece of work. *You* were the one who walked out on *me* and now you accuse me of doing the same to you. Go to hell!" Emma moved so fast her chair fell over. She grabbed her coat and headed for the door before a stunned Hunter even realized what was happening. He ran for the door just in time to see her getting into a cab. It was like the last ten minutes were all in slow motion for Hunter. This was not what he expected to hear. Reality started to formulate—his father was the mastermind behind their break-up.

"Well, that went well, tiger." Hunter turned around, ready to take a swing until he saw Ryan. "Bravo! You really know how to charm a lady." Ryan shook his head and walked over to the table to pick up Emma's chair. "So, I take it you asked her about the break-up?"

Hunter sighed. "Well, I didn't exactly ask. She's right—I'm a pompous ass. I accused her of walking out on me and told her that I wouldn't have a repeat of that for this gala." Hunter slouched in his chair replaying what had just happened in his mind.

Ryan sat down at the once romantic table for two. "Have you ever thought about asking instead of accusing? You know, the whole bees with honey versus vinegar thing? Man, she was raging." Ryan looked directly at Hunter like Emma had only minutes prior. "Hunter, that is something that you *don't fake*. I could see the look on her face. She was so hurt and surprised by your accusation. And I have to say, that part about your jerk-off father fits him to a tee."

"Tell me something I don't know. This doesn't add up. My father told me he never saw her, and it sounded like she never got my letters. He played both of us and was so convincing I believed him." Hunter painfully stared at Ryan.

"If you want my unsolicited advice, I'd say stop analyzing and get your ass over to her place and grovel. Both of you have some sorting out to do." Hunter was about to interject but Ryan continued, "Look, the way I see it is that you have two choices—you can continue down the path of turning into your father *or* you can go after the only woman you've ever loved. And before you take a swing at me, stop and think about what I said. You know I'm right and that I always have your back. I'll clean up this mess—get out of here."

Hunter put on his coat and shuffled to his car, where he sat questioning the events of the evening and those of ten years ago in his mind. Would his father be that cruel? Yes, he would if it meant he got something out of it. Hunter just needed to find out how all this had benefited his father. The Mercedes sped off in the direction of Hunter's penthouse. He knew he should try to talk to Emma, but before he could do that, he needed answers. Hunter wondered if dredging up the past was really the best idea or was it opening Pandora's Box.

CHAPTER 10

———

As the cab pulled in front of Emma's building, she finally realized the enormity of the night's events. She paid the driver and practically ran into the building. When the elevator doors finally closed, she broke down in tears. By the time she was in her condo, she was shaking from crying. She went to the liquor cabinet and pulled out the bottle of Jameson. She poured two fingers of the Irish whiskey into a Waterford tumbler and stared at the amber colored liquid before she took a sip. The whiskey gently warmed her entire body as it slid down her throat. She was pouring another glass when her cell phone rang.

Emma didn't recognize the number and hesitated before answering. "Hello?"

There was dead air for a minute before a raspy voice said, "You're still a whore." The line went dead.

Emma stared at the phone in disbelief before she let it drop on the counter. So many questions were knocking around in her head. Did she imagine this because she was so enraged with Hunter? Her number was unlisted—how would someone get it? She thought the voice sounded like a man's but couldn't be sure. Emma downed the rest of the Jameson in her glass, double-checked the security locks on her door and went to take a shower. She wanted to wash away all the bad memories that bubbled to the surface and blended the past with the present.

While in the shower, her mind relaxed enough to start reviewing the night's events. Hunter had accused her of not contacting him. He thought she had walked out on him. Was he just turning the situation around to make her feel guilty or was there something else that happened? That didn't make sense, even for Hunter. She needed answers and was determined to get them, even if she had to face the lion himself.

Emma crawled into bed and prayed for a dreamless night. She needed to be well-rested so she could focus on whatever was drawing her into this tangled web. Unfortunately, her prayers were not answered. Instead, the intensity of her dreams was off the charts.

Emma was horseback riding in the fields of Hardwicke. There was a stream on the other side of a clump of trees, a place where Hunter and Emma would frequent so they could get away from the world. She slowed the horse to a stop and climbed off the beautiful beast. In the next frame of the dream, she was lying on a pale blue Egyptian cotton blanket next to the stream. Her hands were gently pinned above her head by her partner's muscular hand. His other hand was aggressively exploring, grabbing, and penetrating. She knew that she shouldn't enjoy this, but it was almost addictive.

She couldn't see his face but knew that he was experienced at getting what he wanted. He knew just the right places to touch her to send her into spasms. He pushed her legs open even wider as he roughly thrust his hardness deep into her. Her back arched in ecstasy when he reached climax. His face came out of the shadows with his renowned smug look. "My little whore," he said with a smirk.

Emma woke with a panic. It was four o'clock in the morning. She was dripping in sweat. The sheets were tangled around her almost preventing her from getting out of bed. The nightmare sent shock waves through her brain. She knew that it was her subconscious playing a cruel trick on her based on her confrontation with the past. Emma felt queasy at the thought of that man ever touching her, especially in the special place where she and Hunter had secretly made love. Her body responded with dry heaves. She grabbed the waste basket next to the bed like it was a life preserver.

When she felt stable enough to stand, Emma walked to the window and absently looked out at the city. For the first time ever, she decided to close the drapes. She felt spooked, like someone was watching her, although she knew it was just a result of her nightmare. This monster was now invading her from the grave. Emma's thoughts drifted down a dark path: Philip's body had never been found. She had never told anyone that Philip called her a whore. Could he still be alive?

Emma knew there was no chance of getting back to sleep. She decided to take a shower to wash off the proverbial filth from her terrifying dream. She had brought some work home with her that she had intended to look at last night before she was hijacked by Hunter for dinner. Work always provided a solace for Emma that she couldn't really explain—today she needed that more than anything.

Instead of diving into work, her thoughts drifted again to the blowout with Hunter. She wondered how much Ryan knew about their history. She made a mental note to talk to Ryan if the opportunity arose. He had warned Emma to be careful. Was this what he was talking about? Emma shook her head and muttered to herself, then proceeded to start the day.

Emma walked into the office building at 7 a.m. and almost gave Stan a heart attack. "Ms. Sharpeton! I didn't expect to see you this early."

Emma mustered a smile, "Morning, Stan. Couldn't sleep so figured I'd come in early. I brought you that latte you like." Stan beamed like he had won the lottery when Emma handed him the hot gourmet coffee.

"You sure are something special, Ms. Sharpeton." Stan winked at Emma.

"Stan, you're making me blush," she said jokingly. "Have a good day."

He waved to her as she entered the elevator.

Emma sometimes liked coming in earlier than everyone else. There was a calmness about the office when she was the only one there. It was peaceful and soothing, especially without Ashley bouncing around like she did. It was Emma's time to think—and she knew that she needed that today. Emma's smile quickly faded as the elevator doors opened and she saw Hunter sitting outside her office.

"I'm not even going to ask how you got in here." Emma tried to keep her anger in check.

"I am a very persuasive man," Hunter said flatly.

"Ya, sure you are," Emma said, rolling her eyes.

"Actually, I know Stan from way back. There were a few burglaries at my warehouse down by the docks, and Stan was the one that 'cracked the case' as they say. Ended up being a couple dock hands who thought that they could sell the pharmaceuticals on the street like it was crack."

"I didn't know that. He *is* a good man," Emma said sincerely.

"But we both know that's not why I'm here."

Hunter held his breath.

"Yes, *why* are you here? Rested and ready for round two? And how did you know that I would be here? Oh wait, Stan probably has you on speed dial," Emma barked, bypassing Hunter on the way to her office. She went about her morning routine as she tried to pretend he wasn't invading her space.

"I wanted to apologize about last night." Emma stopped with her daily tasks and began to say something, but she could tell by the look in Hunter's eyes that she should let him continue. "For years, I thought that you had blown me off and honestly didn't have the balls to tell me. You took the easy way out by just not responding. My father convinced me that you were only after my money, and that I was better off without you." Hunter exhaled.

Emma quietly sat in her chair not taking her eyes off him.

Hunter took a deep breath before he continued, "I realized last night that wasn't the case. Your reaction was not one that could've been planned or performed. I also realized by the things that you said we were both led to believe the worst about each other. I strongly believe that my father told the boarding school to destroy the letters that I sent to you. I don't have any proof of this, of course, just a feeling."

Emma tried to interject but Hunter waved his hand at her to let him finish. "We were kids and probably more easily manipulated by the ones who are supposed to have our best interests at heart. I didn't know that you went to my house to try to get my contact details. He never told me. In fact, he told me just the opposite –that you never once came by, which proved you were using me. I don't know how my mother fits into all of this but I plan to find out. What he did to you was appalling, and I am eternally sorry." Hunter sat back in the chair he now occupied across from Emma's desk. He stared blankly out the windows at the city skyline.

Emma couldn't believe what she was hearing. It was surreal. Yet she knew in her heart that Hunter was telling the truth. Even a complete stranger could see the pain on his face, in his eyes. The usual sparkle was not in those eyes this morning, only a deep sadness. Without a second thought, she knelt beside the chair he was sitting in and put her hand on his knee. Hunter looked at her for the longest minute like he was searching the universe for answers.

"Hunter, sometimes the ones we love the most are the ones who hurt us the worst. And first loves are always the hardest. I want to apologize as well. I shouldn't have gone all postal on you last night. I should've given you a chance to explain and I didn't. You always said that I was fiery, and I guess I proved that last night." Emma's tone softened.

Hunter started to say something but knew it was his turn to be quiet.

"We both jumped to conclusions, or at least were led to those conclusions. I can see how much this distresses you. I'm sorry but your father was an awful man. I didn't grow up in the same environment as you so things like this just don't make sense to me."

Hunter interjected in a near whisper, "Did you know I was always jealous of your family? You all were so honest and loving. I wanted to be a part of that family instead of mine."

Emma had never seen Hunter like this before. It was a little unsettling—the confident business conqueror was a little boy who lost his puppy. "How about some tea?"

Hunter laughed as that was what the Brits always used as a cure-all. "Sure, but only if you have English Breakfast tea." The twinkle in his eyes started to come back, even if only slightly.

"Hello! Don't you know anything about me?" Emma began to relax and managed a smile as she led him back to the kitchen area.

"This is a really nice space you have," Hunter said honestly.

"Compared to yours it's the projects," Emma said, grinning.

"Seriously, it's homey and comforting. It's definitely all you." Hunter didn't try to hide his admiration towards Emma.

She blushed slightly. "It is now before the troops get here. Then it will be like Chucky Cheese for adults. They're a great group of creative minds but it can be a bit like running a daycare...very exhausting."

Emma made both cups of tea to perfection under the watchful eye of Hunter. That was one thing she learned from Hunter's housekeeper/nanny—the art of making a proper cup of tea. She handed the mug to Hunter and watched him take in the aroma.

"Pauline was a good teacher," Emma said with a smile.

"Yes, she's great. She is very grounded and a good sounding board when you need it."

"Hunter, let's forget last night happened. We still have a lot to do for the gala, which means we need to find a way to work together, so how about we focus on that?" Emma tried to find middle ground before they were both swallowed up by the past.

Hunter moved closer to Emma so that the already small kitchen felt even smaller. For what seemed like an eternity, he just looked into her emerald green eyes. Then with his free hand, he gently moved a strand of honey blonde hair out of her face and tucked it behind her ear. He stroked her face like it was the first time he was seeing her. It was as though time went into slow motion and all either of them could hear was the beating of their two hearts.

As sudden as the moment started it was interrupted. "Oh my God! I am soooo sorry. I didn't realize you were here yet. And with Mr. Logan. Oh my God! Um, I'll be at my desk if you need me," Ashley rambled before bolting back to her desk.

Hunter muttered under his breath before he said, "Well, I should probably be getting into the office and I know you have a lot of work to do. Thank you for the very nice *proper* cup of tea." Hunter kissed the top of Emma's head before walking to the front of the office.

"How about lunch today?" Emma blurted out before she even realized it.

"I have a client meeting today unfortunately."

Emma felt disappointed, which confused her. "I understand. It was just a thought."

"And a good one," Hunter said, smiling at her. "How about dinner tonight instead? My place around seven? I will have my driver pick you up."

"Your driver? You mean Ryan?"

"Ryan is my second in command. This will be my official driver, mostly because I don't want to deal with Ryan's incessant questions about you. He's like a brother to me but sometimes I wish he had an off switch." Hunter looked at Emma thoughtfully. He noticed how her natural beauty radiated from her.

"Dinner would be nice." A pink hue came over Emma's cheeks. Unbeknownst to her, the office was starting to fill up and many of her employees were witnessing their exchange.

Hunter smiled at Ashley as he sauntered passed her desk. Before entering the elevator, he said to Emma, "Until tonight." Then he stepped into the elevator and disappeared. Those who were in the office all turned to look at Emma inquisitively.

"What? I'm guessing all of you have more important things to do than eavesdrop on a business meeting." Emma hoped that she could hold them at bay and not give in to the office gossip she already knew was happening.

Ashley followed Emma into her office and placed a new cup of tea on her desk. When Ashley didn't immediately move back to her desk Emma said, "I'm assuming you have something on your mind, Ashley?"

"First of all, I don't know what is sexier—that body *or* the accent. Holy cow! Talk about the total package *plus all that money*. If you are going to dinner with him tonight, and forgive me for saying this, I think you need some wardrobe help." Ashley looked her boss up and down.

"First, this is a business dinner. And yes, he's 'uber sexy' as you put it the other day. But this is strictly business. Second, this gala is going to mean, hopefully, great exposure for this company, for all of us. This may mean we get more clients across the country or world. Let's keep the gossip to a minimum, deal?"

"Okay, but there is an office pool on when you're going to marry him. Just saying." Ashley strode back to her desk with a self-satisfied look on her face.

Emma put her head in her hands. Evan had to be the creator of this office pool. She really needed another girls' night out soon. And she hated to admit that Ashley had a point: what the hell was she going to wear tonight?

CHAPTER 11

———

The day flew by for Emma with the typical meetings and conference calls. It was getting down to the wire for the gala and everyone knew it. Emma could tell the stress level of the office had risen over the last few days, especially when she moved from a once a week staff meeting to daily check-ins each morning. Each department was to report on their tasks and if projects were red, yellow, or green. Part of Emma's additional stress was waiting for the *Boston Times* article to be published on her and her company. Part of the anxiety, she figured, was because she didn't want to have any office gossip intrude on the article.

Emma reviewed the project dashboard to obtain a status of each task. The main task that was in the red was the entertainment. They had the typical string quartet lined up for the initial opening cocktails - it was the main entertainment that was lacking. Emma knew they would need to strike a fine balance, given the crowd, of upbeat music and music all could dance to. That meant many of the local bands, like Aerosmith and the Dropkick Murphys, were off the list. James Taylor was always well-received at these types of events, and Emma was waiting to hear back from his people. If he fell through, Emma was going to have to widen her search for bands outside of Boston, like maybe Joe Bonamassa. He had a bluesy rhythm and wasn't too hard core for this crowd. Emma made a mental note to call his people in the morning.

Ashley poked her head into Emma's office and said, "Emma, I'm going to take off. It's 5:30 and most of the office has cleared out. You need to get a move on so you are ready by 7 p.m.! What are you going to wear?"

"Oh crap! I was so wrapped up in trying to nail down the entertainment that I almost forgot about tonight. I really should just cancel and keep working on this stuff."

"No way are you canceling!" Ashley stomped over to Emma's laptop, hit 'Save', and then shut it down all while Emma sat stunned. "Why did you do that?"

"If I didn't do that, you would've come up with a hundred and one excuses as to why you shouldn't go tonight. I decided to take matters into my own hands. Now get your coat, we are outta here!" Ashley crossed her arms, looking smug.

Emma was still a bit stunned—she never knew Ashley had it in her to be so aggressive. Maybe Ashley had a future in this business after all, Emma thought as she put on her coat. The women walked to the elevator in silence; Ashley still very proud of herself. When they reached the ground floor, Emma noticed a black Mercedes parked out front, but it looked different than the one Ryan had picked her up in.

At the same time, her phone rang. "Emma, love, I wanted to let you know that Jared should be outside of your building. He will give you a ride to your condo and then to my place. I didn't want you to think someone was stalking you when he approached you."

"Uh, thanks. I can just walk. It's no big deal." Why did she always seem to get a bit tongue-tied with him?

"I would feel better if Jared was looking after you. This way, there's no chance of you getting spooked and not coming tonight. Cheers." The phone went silent.

Emma looked up to see the man she presumed was Jared and Ashley chatting as both stared at her. Jared was a handsome man in his early 50s with the typical chauffeur uniform and a gentle way about him. Emma didn't notice the slight bulge on his left side that holstered a 9mm handgun.

"Ms. Sharpeton, I'm Jared and I'll be driving you this evening."

"I'm pleased to meet you, Jared. Please, call me Emma." Emma flashed one of her famous smiles to which Jared responded with a slight tip of hat. This was like something out of a movie, she reflected.

Ashley said her goodbyes and was off in a flash while Emma was escorted to the waiting car. She slid into the back seat, but before she could provide directions to her condo Jared broke the silence. "You are at Water's Edge, correct, Ms. Sharpeton?

"Yes, I am. Thank you for driving me," Emma responded.

"It's my job, Ms. Sharpeton." Neither spoke until they reached the condo. Again, Jared opened the door for her and helped her out of the car. He walked her to the front lobby of the building.

"I will wait for you here. Please don't rush. We have plenty of time."

"Thanks, Jared. I won't be that long." Emma felt a wave of pressure knowing Jared would be waiting for her.

Once Emma got to her condo, she began the daunting task of finding an appropriate outfit. She wanted to look smart and casual but wasn't sure what that might be in this situation. It was going to be a cool night so that ruled out any of her dresses. Jeans were too casual and not always comfortable. Emma decided to start with the basics—underwear. Emma went into her closet to the lingerie drawer and pulled out the black and pink lace demi-cup bra with matching panty. Hunter would not see these, but wearing expensive lingerie always made Emma feel good about herself. It was her little secret.

Emma finally settled on a pair of lightweight black summer wool trousers with a dark grey sweater. With the outfit laid out on her bed, Emma jumped in the shower for fifteen minutes and quickly towel dried herself. She did a quick blow dry and applied minimal makeup. As they say, less is more. It was 6:15 so she didn't need to rush but felt bad that Jared was waiting for her downstairs. She took one last look in the mirror and was walking out of her bedroom when she realized she didn't have shoes on. She went back to the closet to check out the options and quickly settled on the black leopard print pumps.

It was 6:30 when she hopped in the elevator to head to the lobby. The doors opened and she saw Jared patiently reading the paper on the lobby couch. When he saw her, he quickly got to his feet and walked towards the door. As he held the door open for her, he commented, "You look very nice. Traffic is light so we should make it to Mr. Logan's penthouse in plenty of time."

Once Emma was safely situated in the backseat, Jared started the car and merged into traffic for the 10-minute ride to Hunter's place. Emma was intrigued by what his penthouse would look like and figured it would probably be like his office—

full of masculinity. She found her thoughts drifting to Jared and how patiently he had waited for her. He had probably done this hundreds of times with Hunter's women.

"What am I thinking? I am *not* one of his women," she silently scolded herself.

At that moment, the car slowly came to a stop in front of one of the tallest buildings in the city. Emma strained her neck to look up to the top floor from the car window. If his place was the penthouse, she figured that you could see all the way to Mount Wachusett from up there. As Jared pulled the door open, Emma jolted back to reality. Once inside the lobby, Emma noticed it was very similar to his office building with lots of glass and marble. There was a front desk with two security guards who looked ex-military. Both men nodded at Jared as he quickly took his leave to park the car.

"Ms. Sharpeton, Mr. Logan is expecting you. I will summon the elevator for you now."

The security guard with a name tag of "Simmons" rose from the desk, put a key into the panel next to the elevator to unlock it and then punched in another code presumably to tell the elevator which floor to stop at. Emma thought the security in her building was good, but this was CIA security good, she reasoned.

The elevator arrived and Simmons said, "Have a nice evening, Ms. Sharpeton." Then the doors closed, and the elevator whisked Emma up to the penthouse. At least this elevator, although extremely fast, didn't make her seasick like the one at Hunter's office. The elevator came to a stop and the doors opened to a magnificent foyer with mahogany floors and modern abstract art on the maroon walls.

As Emma was admiring her surroundings, Hunter sauntered in and said, "Emma, dear, welcome to my home."

"It's beautiful. It's very you," she responded.

"And you haven't even seen the best parts yet. You can put your purse on the table over there, and then I'll give you the grand tour," he said with pride. Hunter tried to contain his excitement with having Emma in his space. He hoped she didn't notice how anxious he really was. It wasn't like he hadn't had women here before, but he felt this was very different.

Emma did as she was told and followed Hunter through a short hallway which then led into an incredible living room space. The floor plan was completely open and had floor-to-ceiling windows with amazing views in every direction. It was a combination of modern and masculine. The hardwoods continued throughout the space, the furnishings were of pale tones and simple esthetics separated the rooms. The see-through gas fireplace added a divider between the dining area and living room area. Off the dining area was a master kitchen that any chef would die to cook in. Emma couldn't remember Hunter ever cooking, so she figured he had people come in and cook for him.

There was also a bar area that seemed to be a replica of a London pub. There were two well-appointed washrooms—one on either side of the space, a small pantry off the kitchen and a gently winding staircase leading up to the second floor. Hunter took Emma's hand and led her up the stairs to continue the tour. Emma's heart was pounding: she was sure that his bedroom would be on the tour. She scolded herself for the second time tonight for even letting her mind drift in that direction.

The second floor contained three spare bed-rooms, all with their own private bathrooms, and the master suite. The master suite had dark wood tone furnishings and grayish-blue walls. There was also the same view as downstairs with the floor-to-ceiling windows and a gas fireplace in one corner of the room. Emma tried not to look at Hunter's bed or let her thoughts drift to the countless women who probably had this same tour.

"Penny for your thoughts, love." Hunter couldn't stop observing Emma.

Emma tried not to blush, "This is magnificent, Hunter. I'm guessing you had a hand in design-ing the penthouse?" She tried her best to keep the conversation general.

Hunter chuckled, "Yes I did. You know how meticulous I am with the details. Come, let me show you the bathroom."

Emma looked at him quizzically until she saw what he meant. This wasn't just a bathroom - it was almost the size of Emma's entire condo. It again had the dark wood cabinetry with dark grey marble countertops. There was a stand-alone shower that was enclosed in glass on all four sides and could easily fit five people. It overlooked the ocean and had more jets from every angle than Emma would have ever thought possible. If she had a shower like this one, she may never come out of it, she fantasized.

"We can try out the shower later if you'd like," Hunter said with the sly smile and twinkle in his eye.

"I thought we were having dinner—not a shower," Emma replied hoping to not seem like her knees would buckle.

Hunter let out a laugh and said, "Let's dine first and then see what happens." Before Emma could reply, Hunter moved her out of the upstairs and down to the main floor. "Please sit and relax. I am going to open a bottle of wine that I have chilling in the fridge."

Emma chose the cream-colored Chenille couch to sit on, although relaxing was out of the question. She still wasn't quite certain why she was here tonight. Hunter seemed more himself than he had in her office earlier that day. He was charming, attentive, and devilishly handsome. All this wreaked havoc on her nerves and her imagination.

Hunter returned with two glasses of a French Sauvignon Blanc. She couldn't read the label for from where she was sitting but guessed it had to be expensive. "Cheers." And both clinked glasses as they took a sip of wine.

"This is really nice," Emma commented with a smile.

"Yes, it is." Hunter replied but Emma wasn't sure if he meant the wine or the evening.

Hunter had prepared a delectable herb roasted pork loin with roasted potatoes and Caesar salad on the side. Emma realized that Hunter could indeed cook. Their conversation stayed on safe topics such as the weather, local news, and the gala. When they both finished eating, Emma insisted on cleaning up the plates. She swiftly cleared the table before Hunter could even stand up.

"Just put them in the sink. Pauline, will handle them tomorrow morning."

Emma tried to hide her surprise that Pauline was still working for the family. "She was always so nice to me at your parents' house in Hardwicke. She still works for you?"

"I didn't have much of a choice. She flat out insisted and there was no way I was going against her." They both laughed because anyone who met Pauline would understand she was a formidable woman.

Both went to the couch as Hunter used a remote to turn on the fireplace and dim the lights. "There are many nights when I sit here looking out the windows without any lights on and just the fireplace going. I hope you don't mind. I don't want you to feel uncomfortable."

"Not at all. It is very soothing, actually."

"How about some after-dinner wine? I happen to have a nice bottle of Hardwicke Winery's version of Riesling."

"Sounds good." Emma's body fluttered not knowing where the evening was headed.

Hunter was back to the couch with two more glasses of wine before Emma even realized. "A toast. To a rekindled friendship."

Emma blinked as she clinked her glass with his. This was all making her head spin out of control. Sitting inches apart, they both sipped their wine in silence as they looked out at the nighttime view. Emma felt the heat radiating from Hunter's body along with the smell of his cologne, which caused her body to tingle.

Hunter placed both wine glasses on the coffee table and held out his hand to help Emma from the couch. Emma wasn't quite sure what was happening, but her heart was pounding. These encounters are going to be the death of me, she thought. Emma didn't know what was racing through her mind let alone his at this moment.

"I know that you have work tomorrow and a lot to do still on the gala. I don't want to be the one responsible for you slacking off tomorrow," Hunter said.

"Yes, it's getting a little late. Dinner was great. Thank you." Emma graciously smiled although she was a bit confused with the sudden end to the evening.

"I'm glad you enjoyed it. I'll call the elevator for you and Jared will take you home."

As they walked to the foyer, the elevator was there open and waiting. Emma took her purse from the table and started walking to the elevator when Hunter suddenly grabbed her by the waist, pulled her into him and passionately kissed her. Her body responded in all the right ways. She dropped her purse and clung to him.

They seemed frozen in time. Hunter moved his hand down her backside as he moved her to the wall. He picked her up so her legs wrapped around him with her back against the wall, which gave his hands the freedom to explore. He moved his hands beneath her sweater tracing her abdomen and her breasts. Then in one single motion, he pulled the sweater over Emma's head and threw it to the floor. For a brief minute he admired her physique before he continued his exploration. Emma moaned at his touch and each time he thrust his tongue deeper into her mouth.

Both were breathing heavily and felt dizzy. Hunter pulled away and said, "I want you right here, right now, but we are still on fragile ground. I don't want to jeopardize anything with you by not thinking things through." He gently put Emma down and gathered her sweater from the floor.

"You want to stop?" For the second time in less than ten minutes, Emma was thoroughly confused.

"*Want* would be a strong word…but I think it's best. Please understand that this is not my nature. But I don't want that with you—the one-nighter." Hunter hoped Emma would understand his feelings ran deep for her and the last thing he wanted was for lust to replace reality.

Emma was still in just her bra and pants. "And if I told you I didn't want you to stop. That I'm a grown woman and I can handle it?"

Hunter sighed, "I'll make you a deal. Let's wait until the gala and see where things are heading."

All Emma could say was, "Sure. If that's what you want." She pulled her sweater on and grabbed her purse from the floor.

"Please don't be mad. I'm trying, for once, to be a gentleman."

"You have succeeded." And with that Emma got on the elevator and was whisked to the ground floor. She didn't even have time to catch her breath before seeing Jared waiting for her.

"The car is right outside. I hope you had a

nice evening."

"Yes, it was nice," she managed.

The two rode in silence once again as Emma tried to process the evening's events. Her phone rang. Hunter. She dismissed the call. Then vibrated, indicating a text, again from Hunter. She shut the phone off and decided to deal with him in the morning.

When she returned to her condo, Emma threw her clothes in a pile on the closet floor and crawled into bed. She couldn't believe what a fool she had been. Although she had no expectations for that night, she still felt hurt and abandoned. And she was mad at herself for taking leave of her senses when he started kissing her. The last two days were an emotional roller coaster for her. Emma knew deep down she didn't want to be on this roller coaster ride anymore. Hunter was too dangerous for her and her sanity.

CHAPTER 12

————

In the morning, Emma absently turned on her phone to see a multitude of voicemails and text messages from Hunter. She wanted to just hit delete but curiosity got the better of her. The voicemails were all basically the same—Hunter apologizing profusely and telling her he was trying to do the right thing even though it was the hardest thing he had ever done. The text messages were all similar - him pleading for Emma to call or text him and he hoped she understood. Emma hit delete and started her busy day.

This was all for the best. They were from very different worlds. Her priority was her career even though her mother would strongly disagree. Emma chuckled to herself at that thought. Her mother was a strong and determined woman, but one that never felt complete unless there was a man in her life. That was definitely not how Emma viewed a complete life.

When Emma got into the office, she made a

preemptive strike, "Ashley, before you ask, the evening with Hunter was all business. Nothing more, nothing less." Emma didn't wait for a response before heading into her office to start prepping for their daily gala check-in meeting. That last thing Emma needed was to be part of the office gossip trail.

The final details were starting to come together nicely, and the rest of the day progressed at a good pace, which she was thankful for. After all the calls and texts the previous night, Emma was surprised that she heard nothing from Hunter. Part of her was upset, although she didn't understand why.

By Friday at 5 p.m., the office was clearing out and almost empty when Emma heard Ashley quietly talking to someone. Emma figured it was Ashley's flavor of the week, picking her up for a hot date. The only thing Emma had a hot date with was a bottle of wine and a movie on the couch. She was completely exhausted from the week's events and even bailed on girl's night. Emma knew she wouldn't be able to deal with the endless questions, especially if she had suggested a different restaurant.

Emma heard a quiet knock on her door before Ashley whispered, "Um…Emma, Hunter's friend, Ryan, is here to see you. What do you want me to tell him?"

Emma let out a sigh. This is all I need, she thought. "Send him in."

"Ryan, you can go in. If you don't need anything else, I am going to head out."

"Thanks, Ashley. Ryan, come in and sit down."

Ryan didn't say anything as he sat in the chair across from Emma's desk. He just looked at her.

"How can I help you?" Emma said, even toned.

"I wanted to make sure that you were all right," Ryan said quietly, not making direct eye contact.

"Is there any reason for you to think I wouldn't be?"

Ryan's voice raised a few notches and his tone was stern. "Emma, don't play coy with me. You haven't answered a single call or text from Hunter, so you knew he was eventually going to send me over here. And for the record, I don't like being the middleman in all this. I honestly have more important things to do with my time than pass love notes between you both in study hall. You two have this crazy, off-the-chart chemistry, and in my opinion, it's toxic for both of you. I warned both of you about this. You don't understand the world he operates in—it's dangerous and you are his Achilles' heel to anyone who wants to come after him." Ryan stopped not knowing if he was getting through to her.

"Are you done?" Emma was seething.

"Yes…for now."

"First of all, I am fine. Secondly, it was Hunter who chose to go down this path. *Not* me. And thirdly,

I am not going to be some pawn in whatever game he is playing. One thing I learned when my father died was that life was too short for games." Emma stared at Ryan as intensely as he was doing to her. She was not going to be intimidated by Ryan or his dramatic dissertation.

Ryan couldn't help but be impressed. He knew Emma had a fire in her soul, but she didn't even flinch like most women would at this conversation. "Okay. I get it. He's an ass, but in this case, from what he told me, he was trying not to be an ass. Look, in other circumstances I think you would be good for him. You seem to bring out a side of him that rarely comes out…the human side. But right now, he has too many enemies who would do almost anything to bring down the king of the mountain. I honestly don't want you to be collateral damage." Ryan began to stand to leave.

"Ryan, I don't need you to fight my battles for me."

Emma and Ryan turned to see Hunter standing in the doorway. Emma visibly sighed. She felt a migraine dancing around in her head. She wanted to run screaming from her office but both men were blocking her way. Emma rubbed her temples as the men started sparring.

Ryan was the first to dive into the ring. All Emma could think was that this was going to end up like Fight Night at the MGM in Las Vegas. "Hunter, you are the one bitching all day that you haven't heard from her. So, yes, I came over here to talk to her and make sure she was okay. And to make sure she understood the stakes. Sue me." Ryan stormed out of the office and hopped in the elevator before Emma or Hunter could respond. They were left standing together in yet another awkward moment.

"Well, you seem to have that effect on people," Emma commented sarcastically.

Hunter wasn't fazed by Ryan's outburst or Emma's sarcasm. "Emma, I want to try to explain."

"No, Hunter, you feel guilty. That's all it is. Look, we had a nice dinner and you chose not to have dessert. That was your choice and your choice alone. Now you get to live with it. I'm fine. Everything is fine between us. We just aren't going to be friends with benefits. Now, if you'll excuse me, I need to get home because I actually have a real date tonight." The last part came out of Emma's mouth unexpectedly and she tried her best to be casual with the little white lie.

"With whom?" Hunter demanded.

"With *None of Your Business*. Have a nice weekend, Hunter." Emma got her coat and briefcase and left Hunter standing in her office, dumbfounded. She had to admit that she was pleased with herself. While her back was to him waiting for the elevator, she let a small smile slide out. They both rode the elevator in silence. When it opened to the lobby Hunter asked, "I can drive you home if you want?"

"No thanks. I'll just walk. We'll talk next week about the final plans for the gala." Emma walked out of the building and down the street towards her condo while Hunter stood on the sidewalk watching her. It was rush hour on a late spring Friday night and the city was buzzing. All Hunter could focus on was Emma briskly walking away from him like he had the plague.

Emma could feel Hunter's eyes burning into her soul until she turned the corner and headed down her street. All she could think about was how much of a pompous ass he was when she almost knocked over a middle-aged man. Emma ran smack into him, and since she was walking with such purpose, she almost bounced right off his chest and onto the ground.

The startled man said, "Oh gosh, miss, are you all right?" He extended his hand to help steady her while she regained her composure.

"I am so sorry! I obviously wasn't paying attention." Emma looked at the man—probably late-40s, distinguished and handsome in that stockbroker kind of way. She could tell he worked out with how hard she had bounced off him.

The man chuckled, "You look like you have a lot on your mind. I'm just glad you bumped into me instead of a taxi or bus." He flashed a smile that relaxed Emma a bit more. Emma nonchalantly looked at his left hand and didn't see a wedding ring or sign there ever had been one, although that didn't mean much these days. She silently reprimanded herself—picking up strangers on the street was not her style. He could be some psycho killer for all she knew.

"Yes, it was a bit of a long week. Again, I am very sorry."

Emma started to walk away when the man said in a sultry voice, "Maybe we will run into each other again." Then he continued on his way without another word.

There was something in his tone that brought up Emma's guard. She wasn't sure what it was or if she was just being paranoid after that confrontation with Ryan. Emma walked the last hundred feet to her building and by the time she was inside, she had forgotten about the distinguished mystery man.

CHAPTER 13

When she reached her condo, her cell phone began singing *Beautiful Day* by U2. She answered the call to the sound of her brother's voice on the other end.

"How are you, love? Just checking in because you've gone off the grid the last few weeks. Mom thinks you've got a guy chained up in your condo and you are doing unspeakable things to him."

Emma's brother, Robert, always could put a smile on her face. Robert was three years older than Emma, extremely handsome and beginning to develop a mix of a Boston and London accent that was very hot to women, from what he told her. He had moved to London for work several years ago, but they still managed to talk once a week. Robert was a tremendously successful investment advisor and worth millions as a result of buying low and selling high. And the one person who could always brighten Emma's day with just a phone call.

"Hi, big brother. Isn't it kind of late in London?"

"The night is still young, my sweet little sister. Now tell me about this bondage man you have hidden away." Emma could hear him laughing at his own joke.

"I think you are watching too many movies. No bondage in my place—well, at least not yet." Emma let out a sly laugh as she bantered with her brother. "How's Sophie? You two still banging your way through London?"

"Sorry, love, Sophie is yesterday's news. I met the woman of my dreams last night."

Emma rolled her eyes. It seemed like Robert was always meeting the woman of his dreams. His relationships would last a month or two and then fizzle. She knew how restless her brother could get—he wasn't the marrying kind. He liked the thrill of the chase, and not the long-term after-effects, which was what made him so successful in the financial world.

"Another love of your life? What does this make? Four in the last seven months?"

"Well, you know you need to kiss a lot of frogs and all that. Her name is Alexa, she's a legal assistant by day and a total vixen by night."

"I don't think I want any details." Emma sighed. She knew her brother was just getting started. The Sharpeton siblings had always been very close and told each other practically everything. Emma just didn't feel like hearing about his latest conquest after such a crappy week in her own life.

Tracey L. Ryan

"All I will say is she is incredibly flexible and vocal. Em, are you okay? You sound a bit off tonight."

"I'm fine. It's been a crappy week. The gala is in crunch time and Hunter is an ass."

She knew that the mention of Hunter's name would set Robert off. Robert thought Hunter was a spoiled little rich kid who had been using his sister. When things ended, it was all Emma could do to keep him from doing some serious damage to Hunter's pretty face the next time he showed up in Hardwicke.

"Don't get me started about that piece of shit! Keep your distance from him. This time you won't be able to stop me from pummeling him. I mean it, Emma." For the first time in a long time, she knew Robert was totally serious. He would be on the next flight to Boston if he knew even a bit of what was going on with her and Hunter. Emma cringed at the thought.

"It's fine. Don't go all nuclear. I'm not a little kid anymore. I can handle myself, and I can handle him. He's quickly learning that just because he's a Logan, it doesn't mean he gets everything he wants." Emma stood her ground partly to calm her well-meaning brother down and partly to remind herself.

"Good. Don't give him an inch or he'll take the universe. You know you can call me if you need anything," Robert said sincerely.

"I know. And I love you for it." The love Emma had for Robert radiated through the phone.

"Fine. I need to get back to my little vixen who has been sitting very patiently on my desk while I've been chatting with you. It's amazing how great I am at multi-tasking."

Emma heard a giggle in the background and shook her head. "Have fun. Be careful. Love you."

"Love you, too." Robert ended the call as Emma could hear a faint groan.

Emma headed straight to the wine fridge and pulled out a bottle of Sauvignon Blanc that was perfectly chilled. So much for a date night, she thought. Her thoughts drifted to Hunter. He probably had several women lined up for the weekend. Emma kept admonishing herself for even thinking of him. She thought she heard the elevator, but that was impossible. Her mind was playing tricks on her thanks to Ryan. Visitors had to be buzzed up. She listened for another minute, shrugged, and walked to the bedroom with her glass of wine in hand. She threw her shoes in the closet and put the wine down on the nightstand. Again, the clothes ended up in the small volcano growing in her closet.

Emma thought she heard another noise, listened for a minute and concluded she was losing her mind as she walked naked into the bathroom. It seemed Ryan had been successful in spooking her. The steam filled the room as the hot water cascaded down her body. She ran her soapy hands over herself, trying to wash away the day. Emma sat on the bench with one leg up on the bench and let the pulsing water splash over her, as she held her head in her hands.

A crash startled her. Definitely *not* her imagination. Someone was in her condo—but how? She was breathing heavily as she stepped out of the shower and grabbed her bathrobe as quietly as she could. Emma left the water running so that whoever was in the living room wouldn't realize she had heard them. She realized her cell phone was on the kitchen counter. "Damn it," she whispered to herself.

She had so many thoughts going through her head. The stranger she ran into just steps from her building, Hunter and his security team or Ryan checking up on her. But nothing could explain how someone got into the condo. You would have to have the key code and only her mother and brother had the code.

Emma stopped next to her bed and reached underneath for the 9 iron she kept there just in case. Although, admittedly, she never thought she'd need to use it. She quietly crept from the bedroom down the hallway into the semi-dark living room. She could see a shadowy figure turning on the fireplace.

"I'm armed and am going to give you until the count of three before your life flashes before your eyes!" Emma shouted as intimidatingly as she could.

The shadowy figure slowly turned around and in his sexy British accent said, "I surrender."

Emma breathed a sigh of relief that it was Hunter before she became furious as to his audaciousness. "What the fuck are you doing in my place?" she screamed at him. Emma couldn't believe his arrogance and the fact he invaded her very private space.

Hunter could see that she was only in a pale pink fuzzy robe and had a golf club in her hand, ready to take his head off. "First, can you put down the club? You are kind of freaking me out." Emma put the club on the couch. "I get that you are pissed at me, but I can explain. I tried calling from downstairs, but you must have been in the shower."

"That still doesn't explain why you are standing in my living room! How did you get in here since you don't have my personal code?"

Hunter replied sheepishly, "Well, I kind of bought this building so I have everyone's codes for emergencies." Hunter had the decency to blush at the revelation.

"You. Bought. This. Building." Emma said it more like a statement than a question. "So, you are stalking me? This is illegal and violates my privacy!"

Hunter knew this was not going well. He had bought the building only as an investment or so he kept telling himself. "I bought it last year. And yes, I didn't tell you because I thought you might react this way. It was an investment opportunity—nothing more, nothing less. No—I am NOT stalking you! I may be a dickhead but I'm *not* a stalker. I have a great deal of respect for women. I just don't always handle things correctly." Hunter was calm and trying to get Emma to calm down.

"Oh my God! You are out of your fucking mind! How did you think I should react?"

"I'm now seeing this was a bad idea. I don't seem to be able to win with you. I screwed up the other night, and I'm trying to fix that except I just made it worse. Look, I'll leave, and this won't happen again. You have every right to be angry. I abused what little trust was between us—I see that now. I'm sorry, really. I just didn't like how we left things between us. Fuck it. I obviously don't know what the hell I'm doing here."

Hunter grabbed his blazer from the kitchen island bar chair and started walking towards the elevator. For the first time, Emma saw Hunter completely defeated. He looked like a little boy. Just before he reached for the elevator call button, Emma said, "Wait. Please."

Hunter turned to see Emma studying him, some of the fury was gone from her emerald green eyes. "Em, you are right. I overstepped my bounds in a big way. The fact is, I'm not used to living within bounds. This is a bit of uncharted territory."

"That is no excuse, and you know it! And don't act like you don't know what you're doing. Every move you make has always been calculated since I've known you. We need to set some ground rules. You can't just show up here. You can't just assume."

"This isn't an excuse—I'm just not used to this. Usually people are falling over themselves to do whatever I want. And, trust me, most are ultimately using me for their personal gain. I just forget what it is like to be human, sort of speak." Hunter let out a heavy sigh like he had the weight of the world on his shoulders. "And sometimes I *am* spontaneous like tonight... Ah, Emma, do you know that your shower is still running?"

"Oh crap! I forgot I left it on." Emma ran back to the master bath to turn off the shower while Hunter waited patiently in the foyer. He could hear her cussing some more and was contemplating going to help. But after how this evening has turned out, he opted to safely wait where he was.

"Emma, is everything okay?" Hunter shouted.

"Fuck! Yes—I just forgot to close the shower door so there's water everywhere." This day is just getting better and better, she thought.

"Do you want some help?" Hunter wasn't sure if he should go help Emma or wait patiently in the living room.

"Can you grab some towels from the linen closet in the hallway?" Emma pleaded.

Hunter did as he was told, which was a completely new experience for him. He smiled to himself as he thought that it was a feeling he liked. "Oh, wow. I'm sorry. This is all my fault." Hunter watched Emma kneeling on the floor mopping up the mess. "Look, go sit by the fire in the living room. This was my fault so I'll clean it up," he said gallantly.

Emma stared at Hunter in utter disbelief and immediately wondered what his angle was. She doubted he had ever cleaned up anything in his life. "Fine," was all she could manage to get out. Hunter rolled up his sleeves and got down on his knees to mop up the water while Emma went to the couch. Hunter was gone for about fifteen minutes before asking, "Where do you want the wet towels?"

"There's a hamper in the walk-in closet. You can just throw them in there. Thanks."

Hunter went into the closet to find mountains of clothes on the floor with more hanging neatly in the custom designed space. He threw the towels in the hamper and noticed he looked a bit disheveled in the mirror. Hunter stood in front of the mirror for a couple minutes wondering where he was supposed to go from here when Emma sauntered into the room.

"Thanks for cleaning up the mess. I have to say, I'm surprised. That doesn't go well with the corporate barracuda image you've built."

"Yes, I'm a bit surprised, too. That isn't something I would normally do." Hunter tilted his head back and laughed. It was contagious and Emma joined in.

Emma noticed Hunter looking around the closet. "Yes, it's a mess. Haven't had time to go to the dry cleaners or do laundry lately."

"Pauline could come over this week and take care of it for you…if that's something you would want." Hunter knew he had to tread lightly.

"I can't ask her to do that. I'll get to it eventually or else I will have to go to work naked." The words flew out of Emma's mouth before she knew it. She wanted to get out of these very tight quarters as quickly as possible.

"You look so beautiful when you blush." In one quick motion Hunter was hovering over Emma, breathing in her scent. She was intoxicating and clouding his judgment. He needed to reel himself back to reality; this was too dangerous a game to play right now.

Hunter's cell phone broke the tantalizing moment. Hunter grumbled, "What?" He listened for a few minutes and then ended the call. "We need to get down to your office - now!"

"What's going on?" Emma said in a panic.

"There's been a break-in. That was Ryan. The police are there now." Hunter turned cold and calculating in seconds. "Go get dressed." It sent a shiver down Emma's spine as she went to find some clean clothes to throw on. Hunter was already calling downstairs to have his car brought around front as he strode back to the kitchen to give Emma some privacy.

CHAPTER 14

E mma and Hunter rode in silence the short distance to Emma's office building. Her head was spinning. Why would anyone want to break-in? Why hadn't the police called her directly? There wasn't any money or anything of real value at the office. Maybe the computers, but anyone could easily go to Staples and buy a cheap tablet. She just hoped that no one was hurt, although she knew she was the last to leave the office tonight.

Hunter held Emma's hand to help her out of the car in front of her building and didn't let go until they reached her office space. When they stepped out of the elevator, all Emma could see were police uniforms hovering in front of her office. Hunter had his arm wrapped around her waist, providing support if she needed it. He always admired Emma's strength but everyone needed a little help every now and again, even if they themselves didn't realize it. Emma walked towards her office in a trance. The blue sea of officers parted, and it was then that she was hit with a proverbial ton of bricks. She would have fallen if it hadn't been for Hunter securely holding her against his perfectly sculpted body.

Ryan's voice broke through the trance she was in. "Emma, I'm so sorry." He exchanged a brief look with Hunter that warned him this wasn't good.

Emma just stood and stared blankly into the world of hate that had been her private domain. Almost every inch of the glass was covered in large, red, block printing with the word "whore." It looked like someone had taken an ax to her desk and chair. Wood splinters were strewn across the floor from the immense power of destruction. The leather chair was barely recognizable, almost as if the culprit had imagined Emma sitting in that spot while he swung the blade. It was like she stepped onto the set of the latest spine-tingling thriller movie, not something that was actually right in front of her.

One of the detectives cautiously approached Emma. "Ms. Sharpeton?" All Emma could do was nod. "I know this is a shock to you, but we are going to need to ask you some questions." He looked to be in his mid-forties, tall and fit with the standard police buzz cut. The detective gave Hunter a nod toward the reception area as a place for them to talk. Emma sat on the sofa with Hunter planted right next to her. The detective spoke calmly, "Ms. Sharpeton, I am Detective O'Reilly and I am very sorry that you had to see this." Emma just looked at him as tears welled up in her eyes. "And I'm sorry that I need to ask you a few questions, but I am going to need your help to catch this guy."

Emma nodded again as she sat there still trying to process the situation.

"Thank you. Have you had any recent threats or anything that seemed out of the ordinary lately? A past romantic encounter maybe?"

Emma said shakily, "No-o-o. Who would do this to me?"

"I honestly don't know. This seems very personal given nothing was stolen and it was only *your* office that was defaced. Have you noticed anyone watching you?"

"No, I'm sorry. I just don't know who or why this would happen. I haven't had any bad breakups or any unsatisfied clients." Emma was starting to gain her composure and her anger was bubbling to the surface. "All I do is work lately, detective. We all left the office tonight around 5 p.m. I stayed a little later to catch-up on paperwork but was gone by 5:30."

"Okay. Mr. Logan, I'm sorry, sir, but I need to ask you a few questions as well." Detective O'Reilly didn't seem intimidated by Hunter.

"I understand," Hunter said coolly. Hunter made a mental note to have Ryan find out everything he could on the detective.

"Where were you from around 5:30 until now?"

"I left my office at 5:15 and drove here to discuss a business matter with Ms. Sharpeton. We left at approximately 5:30, as she stated. Ms. Sharpeton walked home, and I drove to my penthouse. I caught up on some business calls, which can be verified, before I drove to Ms. Sharpeton's condo at around 6:15."

Emma nodded in confirmation.

"Thanks. I just needed to hear you say it. I already knew that your car was parked there during the timeframe in question. And the security footage has you there as well." Hunter raised an eyebrow but didn't say anything. "Mr. Logan, could this be some sort of revenge for a business deal gone bad with you? I am probably grasping, but is your affiliation with Ms. Sharpeton well-known?"

"No, 'our affiliation', as you call it, is not well-known. We are working on the Children's Hospital Gala together, which anyone on the committee would know. Our involvement is strictly business. Anyone who hates me would take it out on me, *not* her."

"And is there a list of people who hate you, as you put it?"

"Detective, I run a multi-billion-dollar enterprise and have done things that some consider ruthless from a purely business standpoint. I am sure there are many who would love to see my ivory tower crumble, but none that I could think of that would wish me or anyone I am associated with any physical harm." Although Hunter understood why the detective needed to ask these questions, it still didn't make him any less angry. He glanced at Emma, hoping she understood why he needed to downplay their relationship. He said a silent prayer that this didn't have anything to do with his latest business venture.

"Well, this guy was very careful. He avoided all cameras and waited for the security guard to go on break. He also had a way to bypass the key card entry system. My tech guys are puzzled on that one. We've dusted for prints, but I'm not expecting to find anything except the staff's. The spray paint was ordinary and can be found at any hardware store. It looks like he used the ax from the fire box in the hallway. There is one thing that does seem odd. Tom, can you bring over the note?" The young officer handed the note to Detective O'Reilly.

Emma and Hunter looked at each other, puzzled while Tom brought a clear plastic evidence bag with a piece of paper in it. The detective handed it to Emma and asked, "Does this mean anything to you?"

Emma's hands were shaking while she read the typed note. "Trash pickup is on Tuesdays." She went pale, and Hunter thought she was going to pass out. He grabbed the bag but looked perplexed.

"Ms. Sharpeton, do you know what this means?"

"Y-y-yes."

The detective knew that to get the most information from a witness or victim, he had to go easy and pull the bits and pieces out of them. "Take your time. Do you need some water?"

"N-n-no. Thanks." Emma took a deep breath and proceeded, "This is what Hunter's father told me when I was younger and went to his house looking for Hunter. He called me a 'whore' and pushed me off the front porch." Emma couldn't keep her composure any longer and buried her head in her hands as she quietly wept. Hunter tightened his arm around her, feeling how her body was shaking.

Hunter cringed at the thought of how his bastard of a father treated Emma. His hands unconsciously balled into fists. He could feel the anger swelling like a volcano that was on the verge of erupting.

The detective immediately turned his attention to Hunter, thinking that he just caught his guy.

"Unfortunately, detective, my father has been dead for a couple years. He died in a plane crash in the Amazon," Hunter said matter-of-factly.

"Who else knew about this conversation between your father and Ms. Sharpeton?"

"I have no idea. My father and I weren't close. Look, I think we've helped all we can for the moment. You have our contact information if you need anything else. I need to take Ms. Sharpeton home." Hunter stood, pulling Emma up with him as if they were attached together.

Detective O'Reilly also rose to his feet. "We'll be in touch. Here's my card if you think of anything else. Ms. Sharpeton, again, I'm sorry that you have to go through this. I promise to do my best to catch this bastard." With that, Detective O'Reilly turned and joined the rest of his team in trying to decipher the events of the night.

CHAPTER 15

Hunter whisked Emma into the elevator and then into his waiting car downstairs. Ryan was already gone by the time they left. Hunter suspected Ryan was running his own investigation into this debacle. They rode in silence back to her condo. Emma didn't leave the comfort of Hunter's arms once. Upon arriving at Emma's condo, he guided her to her bedroom and put her to bed. Although Hunter wasn't a fan of drug-induced sleep, tonight he knew Emma needed the help of a little blue sleeping pill, which would send her to sleep within a few minutes. She didn't want to take the pill, but finally gave in.

Hunter stayed with Emma until she drifted off into what was probably not the calmest sleep she's ever had. Once he heard her rhythmic breathing, Hunter closed the doors and headed to the living room, where he settled in to keep guard. He had no intention of leaving Emma alone tonight.

Hunter was just about to sit on the living room sofa when his phone vibrated. "Ryan, what have you found out?"

"Hey, mate, how is she doing?" Ryan was sincerely concerned.

"I put her to bed with a little help. She's not good. All that shit from my fucking father all came back to the surface. Even in death, the fucking bastard still wreaks havoc. And how the hell did you find out?"

"It pays to have friends in high places." Ryan never divulged any of his connections and Hunter knew better than to ask. "Look, my friends on Boston PD are going to keep me in the loop on this one. I called in a few favors. I checked out that detective, too. From what I hear he's a righteous guy—he's got a good close rate too."

"Sorry, I didn't mean to snap at you. You know that I appreciate your help. This whole fucking thing is just completely fucked up," Hunter said, running his hand through his already tousled hair.

Ryan knew his friend was feeling a mix of emotions, fury at the top of the list. "Hunter, I don't know how to say this so I'm just going to be blunt. They never found your father's body. Hell, they never found the plane in the jungle. What if he's still around? Is it possible, I mean?"

Hunter rubbed his forehead and slumped onto the couch. "Who the hell knows. I can't see him just hanging out in the background though. He thrived on power and money. I would say 'no', but he was nothing but the most cold-hearted, calculating blighter known to walk the Earth…so ya it *could be* possible. Although my head is screaming this isn't him."

"Okay. I tend to agree with you. It's not probable but it's not completely out of the question. Let me call a few friends, see if I can get any intel on his plane crash. In the meantime, I made the executive decision to put a man on Emma 24/7."

Hunter was completely deflated. "Thanks. She's going to hate it, but I don't give a shit."

"Don't worry. We'll figure this out. I'll have some guys board up the office, so the rest of the staff doesn't see it in case they come in over the weekend. And I'll see if we can get it all cleaned up by Monday morning. That'll depend on when the cops release the scene. I know I don't need to tell you this but be careful and take care of her." Ryan disconnected to start his mission of figuring out what the hell was going on.

Hunter threw the phone on the coffee table and kicked off his shoes. Could this be the work of his father? From a diabolical standpoint, absolutely. He had seen his father do unthinkable things in the name of building an empire. Hunter remembered one of the last fights he'd had with his father had been over Emma. Philip's stance basically boiled down to what was in that note: she was no better than trash. Hunter had decided never to tell Emma about his how his father had felt about her back then. Maybe if he had, many things could have been avoided, but that was water under the bridge. Something kept gnawing at the back of his mind about this situation, something he couldn't exactly pinpoint.

Hunter's stomach growled. He hadn't eaten anything for dinner, and it was already 9 p.m. He opened the fridge to find that Emma had a fair amount of food for a single woman and decided to make some tuna on toast. Just as he started to open the can of tuna, Hunter's phone vibrated again.

It was Ryan.

"What did you find out?" Hunter asked by way of greeting.

"When Emma wakes up, ask her about the guy she was talking to in front of her building tonight on her way home. There isn't a clear shot of him. He seemed to know how to avoid the camera. They chatted for a couple minutes after she literally bumped into him. Like I said, can't see the face, but he looked a bit too bundled up for yesterday's weather. Not sure if that was to throw us off as well."

"Must have been right after I saw her. She's still asleep. I'll ask when she wakes up." Hunter mixed the tuna while talking. As a way of an explanation for the noise, Hunter told Ryan.

Hunter could hear Ryan's belly laugh through the phone. "Ok, Mr. Domesticated. I'll leave you to it. But, seriously, try to get a description out of her. This just seems too coincidental for my internal radar." Ryan ended the call and continued scrolling through video footage. Boston, like many cities after the 9/11 attacks, had installed thousands of video cameras across the city. Although many privacy activist groups were irate, they helped keep Bostonians and visitors safe.

Hunter made what he thought was a damn fine sandwich. He put everything on a tray and tip-toed towards Emma's bedroom. He paused before opening the door; Emma was crying softly. He knocked gently with his free hand. "Can I come in? I made you a bloody fine sandwich." Hunter could hear her sniffling. It felt like a dagger piercing his heart. Emma didn't say 'no', so he opened the door.

Emma was sitting up in bed, trying to gain her composure as best she could. In almost a whisper she said, "I'm not hungry." Hunter walked to the nightstand on her side of the bed and placed the tray on top of it, careful not to scratch the wood. He sat on the side of the bed, stroked her face, and tucked her silky blonde hair behind her ears.

"I think you should eat something—even if it is just a couple bites. I slaved in the kitchen and it's the least you could do," Hunter whispered. He flashed his famous smile, hoping it would help lighten the mood.

Emma reached over and took one-half of the sandwich as she realized she was hungry. "Thank you," she said faintly. "This is actually good."

Hunter pretended to be insulted and patiently waited for some sort of direction from Emma as to what he was supposed to do next. These were not situations he was comfortable in. His immediate reactions were rage at the person who had done this hideous act and absolute protectiveness of the woman who now and always owned his heart.

Emma sat in a haze, just going through the motions. Each time Hunter looked at her and saw the defeated look on her usually strong face, it was like a part of him died. The rage was starting to boil to the surface again, and he knew that now was not the time and place to explode.

Luckily, he could hear his phone vibrating in the other room and quickly excused himself. "I'll be right back. Try to take a few more bites," Hunter said before kissing her head and closing the door to her bedroom.

Hunter didn't recognize the number on the screen. "Hello?"

"Consider this a warning, Mr. Logan," said the distinctly male voice on the other end of the phone before the call ended.

Hunter immediately called Ryan who was still sifting through video surveillance footage from the office building and surrounding streets. "Hey, bro. What's up?"

"I need you to trace a call that was just made to my private cell phone. Call me back with what you find." Hunter ended the call to let Ryan perform the task at hand. Ryan knew not to take offense with Hunter's abruptness—it was part of his personality.

"How the hell did someone get my private number?" Hunter pondered. He knew you could find out anything on the internet and the world had gone hacker crazy, so it was possible that someone with the right skills could have found the number. He had more questions than answers at the moment, which was unnerving for him. Why had Emma been targeted? Why is someone sending a warning to Hunter? Hunter had the uneasy feeling that this dangerous game was just getting started, and he did not like being a pawn. He was used to being the hunter and not the hunted.

Ryan called Hunter back within five minutes without the answers he knew Hunter was looking for. "Sorry, buddy. Call didn't last long enough to get the trace. All I can tell you is it originated from somewhere on the East Coast. Could be anywhere from Bangor to Key West. Now are you going to tell me *what the hell* the phone call was about?"

"It was some sort of warning. And, no, I didn't recognize the voice. And the only thing I do know was that it was a guy's voice—and not computerized—it was real. All he said was to 'consider this a warning.' I don't think the recent events and this phone call are a coincidence."

"I agree. Looks like Emma's break-in *wasn't* random. Not that we really thought it was. *And* it looks like this definitely involves you. I have to admit - I don't like how this is shaping up."

"I know. This is personal somehow. I just need to connect the dots - soon."

"Ya, well, don't wait too long. I think this guy is just getting warmed up. Maybe it would be a good time to take Emma to your little Bahamian retreat."

"Trust me, it's crossed my mind, but you know she's not going to leave town this close to that damn charity gala. That is her pride and joy, and I also don't want to rob her of the glory for all the work she's put into it. The gala may be what this bloke is gearing up for, though. Let's double security at the event just in case."

Ryan agreed. "It makes sense. Let's talk tomorrow morning. Give me a little time to do some more digging and see where we are. If this asshole thinks he can get to you through Emma, that's your Achilles' heel, my friend. Which means she will be bait at this shindig no matter what we do." Ryan shut down the call before Hunter could get more riled up.

CHAPTER 16

H unter didn't want to leave Emma alone for too much longer, but he needed more time to think this through. Ryan would be able to do a lot more digging than he could, given the former spook's unmentionable resources. What Hunter needed to do was create a list of his enemies and then figure out who on that list would have the boldness and intelligence to play a game like this.

Hunter heard soft footsteps coming towards him from the bedroom along with dishes lightly clinking. As he turned, he saw Emma tentatively approaching him. She wore a silk robe and her eyes were bloodshot. She didn't say anything as she placed her dishes in the sink. All Hunter could do was come behind her and wrap his arms around her. For those few minutes, they stood entwined not speaking, only listening to each other's hearts beating. If this were any other situation, he would be untying the robe and caressing her very naked body.

Emma was the first to break the moment. "I'm better now. This was just a shock." She turned to face him; Hunter's arms still wrapped around her. "I've now moved onto the anger phase. I don't know why anyone would want to do this to me, but I will find out *and I will* hold them accountable. They tainted something that is personal to me and they're not going to want to see how I react when they are caught." Her voice was steady and cold as ice, so much so that it gave Hunter a slight chill. He was surprised given her current state of mind that she allowed him to continue holding her.

Anger was good—that was something he could handle. "I don't know why anyone would do this to you either, but I *promise* that I will find out. Ryan has been hard at work trying to figure out what's going on." Hunter tilted her head upwards so that their eyes would meet. "I'm asking you to trust me and not do any sleuthing on your own." It wasn't really a question and Emma knew he could be as determined as she.

"I trust that you and Ryan will do everything possible to find this asshole. I promise not to go and do anything stupid." Emma knew that she needed to let Hunter and Ryan help with this. They had resources she didn't have, and they needed to work together to catch this lunatic.

"You've had a traumatic few hours, and I think you'd be better served getting some rest."

Emma cocked an eyebrow. "Better served?"

"Probably the wrong verbiage. You need time to process all of this. We both do. And I need to strategize our options," Hunter said, acting like this was another merger/acquisition. Realizing his cold demeanor, he bent down and kissed Emma's temple before he ushered her towards the couch.

Emma sighed as she sat on the couch. "You're probably right. I've always been in control...until this. It threw me for a loop." She looked thoughtfully up at him.

"Why don't you watch some mindless TV? I've got some calls to make. May I use your office?" he asked as he draped the sage-colored chenille blanket over her.

"Are you going to call Ryan for an update? I'm not a piece of Wedgewood china, ya know. I won't break. You can talk in front of me." Emma's natural defensiveness went into overdrive.

"Let me do my thing and then maybe we can watch a movie. Sound good?"

"Fine. Just know that I'm a part of this whole thing and I have a right to know what's going on." As Hunter started to head toward Emma's office, Emma said quietly, "Hunter...I'm glad you are here with me."

Hunter debated with himself regarding the warning phone call and thought it best to leave that part out for now. He knew that Emma was going to be beyond angry when he finally did tell her, but until he figured out what was going on it was a need to know basis. He wasn't sure how quickly he'd be able to connect the dots of this dangerous game. Maybe it was all coincidence, but odds were stacked against them, and it wasn't a bet he'd take in Vegas.

Hunter noticed how broken Emma looked as Meredith Brooks' song *Shatter* played in his head. A far cry from the vigorous woman he'd seen over the last few days. To see her like this was killing him inside, and he secretly vowed to rip this bastard limb from limb. "You will absolutely be involved in whatever we find out," was all he managed to say without over-promising.

Emma settled into the couch, satisfied with Hunter's response, and began watching *Jurassic Park*. She quickly became lost in the violence of enormous creatures from a past world, terrorizing the unsuspecting visitors to their island. Hunter watched her a few more minutes to make sure that she was preoccupied and then strode down the hallway to Emma's home office.

Hunter stopped inside the doorway, admiring the tasteful décor. It wasn't too feminine or masculine. There was an exquisite writing desk, matching credenza, and bookcases. A brown leather couch provided a softer touch to the room along with a red & cream-colored Persian-style rug. He smiled to himself as these would be things that he would pick out for himself. Even the accents, like the old-world style globe on the credenza and the brass touch lamps on either bookcase, fit the style perfectly.

Hunter sat in the high-back leather chair behind the desk and dialed Ryan's cell phone number. After several rings, Ryan gruffly answered, "What?"

Hunter realized that Ryan didn't recognize the phone number. "It's Hunter. Find anything yet?"

"Where are you calling from?" Ryan asked suspiciously. His internal radar was ultra-sensitive given the issue at Emma's office, and he didn't like that he didn't immediately recognize this number.

"Sorry, mate. I'm at Emma's—this is her home number." Hunter could appreciate Ryan's suspicious mind—it had helped him on more than one occasion and he hoped it would again this time.

"Gotcha. How's she doing?"

"She's a tough one. And someone that this guy should be fearful of. She's gone into her T-Rex mode."

"Her *what* mode?"

"Sorry, she's on the couch, watching *Jurassic Park*, and I have dinosaurs on the brain."

"Great flick. Love how those things just rip everyone apart. Anyway, I've got a couple of guys doing some research for me. Not sure we are going to get much over the weekend. One thing we do have is that this guy was very careful—*too* careful if you ask me."

"How so?" Hunter absolutely did not like where this was heading.

"As you know, he knew exactly where all the cameras were, so we never got a shot of his face. And it looks like he was in some sort of disguise. I can't even get a clear read on his height, weight or skin tone. *Then*, there's the fact that there was not a single fingerprint that was out of place. No hairs, fibers, or DNA. This has 'pro' written all over it. But what I don't get is why a pro would be into vandalism—not usually their style unless it's part of a bigger job." Ryan let Hunter take all this in, knowing the wheels inside his brain were turning at lightning speed. This was starting to head in a specific direction and couldn't be chalked up to some prank or drug addict.

"This is *not* what I wanted to hear. I was literally praying this was some punk kid. Bloody hell!" Hunter leaned back in the chair and rubbed his temples with his free hand. Ryan knew to wait for Hunter to finish his thoughts before interjecting. "What the fuck is going on? There is an intersection point here that I can't figure out. And I have a feeling this is just getting started."

"Agreed. Look, I'm going to see what else my guys can dig up. I also want to trace her steps over the last few days." Ryan hesitated slightly. "I'm going to have to dig into her personal life: phone records, emails, texts, etc. Just warning you in case

I find something that may be unexpected." Ryan tried to position that as delicately as he could. He hated digging into people's lives that he knew and would never do it unless absolutely necessary. He didn't want Hunter to go ballistic because should some romantic liaisons come to light.

"Ryan, I appreciate your discretion. At this point, all I care about is getting to the bottom of this. Who she may have slept with is irrelevant. Call me on my cell as soon as you have anything," Hunter said as he disconnected. This was going down a path he didn't want to acknowledge. In reality, Hunter knew it would bother him if Ryan uncovered any trysts Emma had. Jealousy wasn't something he was used to feeling.

Hunter pushed the thought from his mind and opened his laptop to in hopes of distracting himself by catching up on emails. One of the emails was from Unknown Sender, which raised a red flag. It was relatively easy to block your email address, no different than blocking your phone number. Hunter clicked on the email. He started to get a sick feeling as an image of Emma appeared on the 17-inch monitor. The bastard had gotten into her apartment while she was asleep. There was a play button icon, which meant there was video. Hunter nearly hit delete but forced himself to watch. As the two-minute video played, Hunter almost threw up in the wastebasket. Emma had been sleeping with the silk sheet loosely around her. She was in dreamland and completely unaware that her personal space had been invaded by some monster getting his thrills from Hunter's reaction.

There was a voiceover to the video, which must have been added after it was taken. Hunter recognized the voice immediately; the same one that called him a few hours ago. "Look at how close I am to your piece of trash. I can just imagine what it would feel like to touch her right now. This is another warning. She's lucky for now but might not be the next time."

Hunter played it three more times before calling Ryan.

Before Ryan could even answer Hunter said tersely, "I just received an email from an anonymous source with a video. I'm emailing it to you now. I need to know where it came from. Now!" Hunter disconnected without giving Ryan the opportunity to say a single word. Ryan would understand as soon as he saw the video.

Fifteen minutes later, Hunter's cell phone vibrated with Ryan on the other end. "You aren't going to like this. This guy is better than good. I can't get any specifics: no location, IP address, nada. I need to see if one of my former colleagues can find anything. She was a hacker before we recruited her. Okay to proceed?"

"Yes. Just don't let this video go any further. And this stays between us." Hunter disconnected once again to let Ryan do what he was paid handsomely for. Emma was somehow the focal point in this whole strategic game. What Hunter couldn't figure out was why and how his father fit into all this. Could Ryan be right that his father was still alive, and this was revenge? But revenge for what? Growing the company to twice the profit margins? Or was this more personal? Questions ran through Hunter's head without a single answer.

Hunter's train of thought triggered a memory buried deep in his past as he leaned back in the chair. His father had never known the definition of love; he only knew dominance. When Hunter was 10-years-old, Philip had decided it was time for some father-son bonding. Hunter couldn't wait. It was the first time his father showed any real interest in him. They rode their horses to the back twenty acres of their estate in Hardwicke. The terrain was intense with trees, rocks, and uneven ground. Hunter struggled to keep up with Philip, who knew this area well. The next thing Hunter knew was that he and the horse were on a downward spiral after tripping on a rock. Hunter was thrown about fifteen feet from where the horse landed. When his father trotted over, he silently took the rifle that was attached to his saddle and shot the horse. Hunter, covered in dirt with scrapes and bruises, burst into tears as he looked up at his father's face asking. "Why?"

The only words his father spoke were: "Now you know what happens when you are weak. You better get up; you have a long walk back to the house." With that, Philip had turned his horse around and galloped back towards the main house, leaving Hunter to walk the three miles by himself.

Hunter's phone vibrated again shaking him back to reality. Another unknown caller. "I assume you saw my movie. Welcome to the game, son." The call ended in less than ten seconds. Hunter had a very uneasy feeling as he called Ryan.

"Ryan, the bastard just called my cell again. We need to…"

Ryan interrupted him, "Yes, I know. I've been having your phone tapped just in case. Guys like this want to get your reaction. They want you to know they can infiltrate your life and you're helpless to stop them. Unfortunately, the call was too short, still on the East Coast though. And my friend has the email. She'll get back to me within twenty-four hours."

"We need to get this guy soon before this goes to the next level." Hunter's blood pressure was off the charts with rage.

Ryan could tell his best friend was deflated and worried, emotions that were foreign to both of them. "I know. I'm working it as quickly as I can, buddy. I'll call as soon as I have something."

Hunter stared at the phone as Ryan disconnected. He needed to convince Emma to stay with him until this was sorted out. The big question was how to do this without telling her the real reason. Another secret he would have to keep.

CHAPTER 17

———

Hunter shut down his laptop and solemnly walked back towards the living room where sadistic dinosaurs were having a feeding frenzy. Emma's head popped up from the pillow. "All done with your calls?"

"For now. I thought I'd come see how things were in here." Hunter picked up Emma's legs and sat down on the couch letting her stretch out on top of his lap. He sighed as he looked at her, taking in those big, beautiful eyes and the curves of her face. She was unaware of the increased danger—a fact that Hunter wanted to shelter her from as much as possible. The image of the video crept into his mind until the screaming on the TV jetted him back to reality.

Hunter couldn't help but notice the openness of the condo. Every room had its drapes completely open, which under normal circumstances would be picturesque. "Do you always leave all your drapes wide open at night?" Hunter tried to probe gently.

"Most of the time. I don't like to feel closed-in. Why?"

"For the time being, let's close them." Hunter tried to act casual.

"You do realize that we are on the top floor?" Emma said, perplexed.

"Everyone has drones these days so you never know what will end up on the internet. Given tonight's events…" He let his words hang in the air.

"Is there a reason you're being paranoid?"

"I prefer to call it being cautious. We don't know who we're dealing with or why. And I take your safety very seriously."

Emma tried to stifle a yawn without much success.

"You should really rest some more. Why don't you try to get some sleep? We can continue this conversation later."

"I'm fine, really. Although every muscle in my body hurts."

"That's due to stress, and I'd say you've met your quota for the day. Come with me," Hunter insisted as he held his hand out to help Emma off the couch. Emma reluctantly took his hand as he gently pulled her to her feet. For a moment their eyes locked, and they were in their own world far away from the ugliness.

Hunter broke the moment and led her back to her bedroom. He pulled the sheets open and gestured for her to slide under them. She did so without argument as he drew the drapes shut. "Now sleep, my precious kitten," Hunter said as he bent down and kissed her forehead. She smiled up at him and got comfortable as he closed the door behind him.

Just as Hunter entered the living room, his phone vibrated. "Ryan, what do you have for me?" Hunter was impatient on a good day - this was almost killing him.

"Dude, did you know that Emma's father worked for your father in some secret lab?"

Hunter was bewildered. This was something he hadn't known, not that he knew a lot about his father's businesses back then. Still, this tidbit of information should've popped up when he was dismantling his father's legacy. There had been no mention of any secret lab or projects.

"Huh? That can't be right. I never found any indication of secret labs or projects, let alone that Mr. Sharpeton was employed at one." Hunter was genuinely perplexed.

"I'm doing more digging to confirm. It was very well hidden and probably not something any of your staff would have been able to find easily. My colleague stumbled across some files that on the surface looked like boring reports but she noticed they were highly encrypted behind-the-scenes. I'm no techie so I only caught half of what she was saying but bottom line is, they were there and difficult to access, which drew her curiosity," Ryan paused to let that sink in with his best friend. He could hear Hunter sigh heavily on the other end of the phone and took that as his cue to continue. "She found a lot of scientific mumbo-jumbo that neither of us really understood *but* the one thing we did understand is that this lab was only known to two people...*your* father and *Emma's* father. *And* it had something to do with cancer research."

Hunter thought about all of this and finally said, "My father was dabbling in pharmaceuticals—he saw it as a high-potential business. Emma's father was some sort of chemist, so theoretically it makes sense. Strange that I hadn't heard of this before now. Though, I'm not sure what this has to do with our current situation or why you'd be looking into my father's past business dealings." Hunter ran his hand through his hair and tried to comprehend this new information.

"I'm not sure if it does have anything to do with what's going on, but I thought it was an interesting tidbit of information that was kept under tight lock-and-key. Emma's background and lifestyle check led to some old emails her father sent, including one with a file attachment. All he told her was to keep this file for him as a backup—he was having computer issues. Three weeks after he sent that email he died in that car accident. May be coincidence, but you know I don't believe in coincidences."

"The pharmaceutical market is highly competitive, which is probably why my father would have had such tight security around any research and development," Hunter sighed. Every turn they took led them in another direction. It was like being in a cornfield maze. "Not sure how her father, and mine for that matter, fit into this puzzle. Keep digging. I want to know as much as we can before I involve Emma."

"Dude, I know what you're saying, but here's some advice: *Don't* keep secrets from this woman for too much longer. She seems like the type that, um, how can I say this, would make a volcano erupting seem tame in comparison."

"I know," Hunter said thoughtfully as his mind drifted to Emma's fiery personality.

"I'll call you when we find out more. Keep a close eye on her. I have a bad feeling about all this. Maybe see if you can get her out of the city for a few days, go to your parents' estate in Hardwicke or something." Ryan hung up and began his covert operation to find all he could about the Logan and Sharpeton families' secrets.

Hunter put his cell phone back on the desk. The gala was fast approaching, and he knew Emma would never leave this close to it. Panic suddenly overtook Hunter as he thought of the gala. What if all this was working up to that event? Everyone knew it was being hosted at his headquarters. Security would be tight, but not impenetrable, and both he and Emma would be there. An attack could come in any form: gunfire, bombs, chemicals. He shook his head. His mind was heading to farfetched fiction. Or was it? These types of things were all over the news every day, although mostly in other parts of the world. But it was still plausible to have homegrown terrorists. And what better way to bring his empire crashing down?

Hunter clasped his hands behind his head as he leaned back in the chair and stared at the ceiling. There were just too many wild possibilities and not enough information to make an informed decision. This was something that Hunter was not used to. He was very calculating and strategic, not a fly-by-the-seat-of-his pants type of guy. Yet, every road seemed to be leading back to his father. He was about to get up to get a drink, when he heard Emma in the kitchen.

Hunter soundlessly walked to the kitchen and leaned against the wall for a moment as he secretly admired her. He smiled to himself as his thoughts drifted to the countless times he had called her stubborn. Hunter hated lying to her but knew that for the time being it was the best way to keep her safe.

"Did you sleep?" Hunter said in the most soothing voice he could muster.

"Oh, hi. I didn't see you there. Sorry—just not used to there being someone else here besides me."

She blushed slightly. "I dozed off and on and then was a little thirsty, so I decided to get up. Have you been working?"

"Yes, kitten, working on making sure nothing happens to you." But Hunter knew he couldn't say that. "Just catching up on a few things. Nothing that won't keep," he said as he flashed her a sympathetic smile. "How about I make you something to eat?"

"I'm not that hungry. What time is it?"

Emma sounded completely wiped out and fragile to Hunter. "It's almost 1:30 a.m. If you aren't hungry, you really should try to get some rest. Ryan has a crew working at your office all weekend to repair the damage by Monday morning."

"Thank you," Emma managed to say as a shiver ran up her spine. This whole situation was surreal: Hunter being in her apartment, the break-in at the office, and the million-dollar question of why someone would do this to her. She could only imagine what both Hunter and Ryan were thinking right now, although she didn't even know the pieces of the story Hunter and Ryan had been finding. It was a very dangerous scavenger hunt.

Hunter sensed her uneasiness. "Kitten, none of this is your fault. You know that, don't you?" Before she could answer, he engulfed her in his arms, with her head leaning on his chest, listening to his heartbeat. "Come on. Let's get you back to bed. I'll sleep on the couch."

Emma didn't have the energy to argue with him or tell him that she really wanted him to stay with her instead of the couch. She felt safe with him; he wouldn't let anything happen to her. Even though she was completely exhausted, there was something nagging at the cobwebs in her brain about this whole situation. No one, not even Hunter, had known what Philip had said to her so many years ago. How is it possible that it was the exact same words used to defame her office?

Hunter eased her into bed and tucked her in under the covers. She watched him as he checked again to make sure the drapes were drawn so not an ounce of sunlight would peak through. Before leaving her to the dark dreams she was sure to have, he brushed the back of his hand across her cheek and bent down to kiss the top of her head. Under normal circumstances, she would have been more aggressive and taken the situation under her control. Neither of them spoke as he closed the bedroom door and headed to the living room.

In complete darkness, except for the faint light under the door from the hallway, Emma fell into a deep sleep more quickly than she thought she would. The dreams started almost instantly, taking her back to Hardwicke and the life she used to have. Even in sleep she knew that the monsters would eventually get her.

CHAPTER 18

Hunter was restless and anxious as he wandered around Emma's condo. He was quite impressed with the décor and furnishings. Considering what a control freak that Emma was, he knew without asking her that she planned the space down to the last knickknack.

Before settling himself on the couch, he made sure his phone was on vibrate so Emma wouldn't be disturbed by Joe Bonamassa's *Just Got Paid* ringtone. This whole situation nagged at Hunter. Sometimes sleep helped him uncover the dark passages in his mind that eluded him in consciousness. Hunter stripped down to his boxer briefs and pulled the chenille blanket over him as he tried to get comfortable.

Within minutes Hunter was headed to a state of unconsciousness, lightly snoring. His dreams took him to Hardwicke and Emma. They were in the horse barn settling the horses back in after a ride. He could see his father there as well but couldn't make out what he was saying. Emma seemed uneasy as she clung to Hunter. His father let out a belly laugh as he pointed at Emma. As quickly as the dream came it left and he moved on to other unsettling dreams for the rest of the night.

The sun's magnificent rays shone through the window like they were a path to the heavens. Hunter stirred, a bit disoriented as he opened his eyes. He quickly realized where he was as he sat up on the couch. He looked at his cell phone to see that it was only 7 a.m. He'd received a text message from Ryan saying the office cleanup was on schedule and there was no other news to report. Hunter felt a wave of disappointment but knew that these things took longer than the hour as seen on TV cop dramas.

Hunter strode to the bathroom in the hall to splash some water on his face and relieve himself. As he looked in the mirror, he wondered what ghosts were beginning to surface. He vaguely remembered the dream about his father and felt uneasy. He would protect Emma at all costs, but this was going to be a monumental task.

After he woke up more, he tip-toed to Emma's room and listen at the door. He thought he could faintly hear her breathing, which meant she was still sleeping. Under different circumstances, Hunter would have thrust the door open in hopes of a morning quickie. Just the thought of waking up next to Emma made his body react. "Down, boy," he whispered to himself.

At that moment there was a soft knock on the front door. Immediately, Hunter went into defensive mode. As he approached the door, he looked for some sort of weapon. The best he could do was to grab the eight-inch chef's knife from the block on the counter. When he peered through the peep hole, he breathed a sigh of relief as he unlocked the door.

"Morning, dude," Ryan said, looking at Hunter standing there in his briefs holding a knife. "Interesting outfit. Not sure the accessory is right to set the mood." Ryan chuckled.

"Very funny," Hunter said unamused as he closed and locked the door behind Ryan. In hindsight, Hunter realized that a criminal wouldn't knock and felt a little silly.

"Emma still sleeping?"

Hunter nodded.

"Guessing she was tired after last night and rightfully so," Ryan made sure that the double-meaning did not fall flat on Hunter as he smirked.

"I slept on the couch, if you must know."

"Sure. None of my business." Ryan held up his hands in mock defense. "Look, I only have a few minutes before I head to Emma's office to get the work crews going. Just wanted to check in to see how she was and to let you know my contacts are working this thing hard. No stone unturned."

"Thanks. Something is off about this whole thing. I just can't get my head wrapped around it."

Ryan concurred. "It all keeps coming back to your father. But that seems just a little too convenient. I feel like we're being led in his direction, and that doesn't sit well."

"Agreed. Thanks again." Hunter really did feel gratitude towards Ryan. He knew, even with vast resources at his disposal, he still wouldn't be able to solve this without the help of his best friend.

"Have you broached the subject about her getting out of Dodge for a few days?" Ryan thought this would be the safest course of action until he could figure out what was going on.

"Not yet. I'll think of something, even it means I sleep on her couch for the foreseeable future." Hunter didn't look forward to this conversation with Emma.

Ryan smiled and winked as he headed to the door. "I know that will be a big sacrifice for you." Before Hunter could throw something at Ryan, he was out the door and safely whisked away in the elevator. As Hunter closed the door, he heard Emma behind him in the kitchen. For the first time in his life he felt a bit embarrassed since he was only in his underwear.

"Morning, love."

"Hi. Who was just here?" Emma looked around but only saw Hunter.

"Ryan came by to let me know he's heading to your office to get the work crews started. He doesn't have any other news though."

Hunter paused and Emma searched for something to say. Given they were both barely dressed, the moment was awkward for each. Emma could feel the heat between them. This was not what she needed clouding her judgment right now. Hunter stood directly in front of her. She desperately wanted to reach out and touch him. Before she could act, Hunter abruptly walked to the couch and grabbed the pants and shirt he wore last night when her world was turned upside down. All she could do was watch him dress in her living room with a pang of disappointment.

"There are extra towels and toiletries in the guest room bathroom if you want." Emma tried to hide her disenchantment.

"Thanks. I'm going to take a quick shower. I don't need to remind you *not* to open the door for anyone." Hunter turned and headed to the spare bathroom at a fast pace, almost running away from her.

When he got into the bathroom, he breathed a sigh of relief. If he had stood there another minute, he would have done something he would have regretted. He stripped off his clothes as he turned the shower on and waited for the water to heat up. Within a minute, he stepped into the steam filled all-glass standup shower and let the water just slide down his body. As he lathered up the soap, his mind again drifted to Emma half-naked in the kitchen.

Hunter quickly turned the water temperature down a few notches to cool his imagination.

Emma heard the shower come on as she was making herself a cup of English breakfast tea. Before her mind could wander into forbidden territory, her cell phone rang. Her heart began to beat faster and her palms were sweaty. Tentatively she answered it. "Hello?"

"Ms. Sharpeton, this is Stan from your office building."

She breathed a sigh of relief. "Good morning, Stan. I didn't realize you worked on the weekends."

"I don't normally but the other guy got sick. The reason I'm calling is there is a guy named Ryan here with a work crew to do some remodeling of your office. Just checking to see if that's okay."

"Yes. I'm sorry—I forgot to let the security office know. Just some minor updates over the weekend." Emma sighed in relief.

"No worries, Ms. Sharpeton. Just didn't want to let strangers into your space." Stan was glad that he called to verify.

"I really appreciate it. Thanks for calling. I'll see you Monday morning, Stan." Emma tried to sound cheerful.

"You bet. Have a nice weekend."

When Emma hung up the phone, she realized that her hands had been shaking. Ryan had better find out what was going on soon or she might have a nervous breakdown, she felt.

Hunter picked that moment to unknowingly startle Emma, who was lost in her thoughts.

"Sorry. I didn't mean to startle you." Hunter stood in front of Emma, this time completely dressed and looked refreshed. "I'd like to talk to you about something."

Emma frowned. "I'm not going to like this, am I?"

"Probably not, but I do think it's for the best. I want you to stay with me for the next few days." He could tell she was getting ready to protest. "I know it's an inconvenience. I'd like for Ryan to install a state-of-the-art security system here and it'll be easier if you weren't here."

Emma looked into Hunter's eyes and could see how worried he was. The normally sparkling sea of blue was cloudy with concern. "Okay. It probably is about time I got one anyhow. And knowing Ryan, it'll be better than the White House has." She gave Hunter a smile that made him speechless for a second. "So, yes, I'll take you up on your offer."

"That was *way* too easy. I've been practicing my rebuttals to your protests all night. Hardly got a wink of sleep. And all for nothing." Hunter was astonished.

"Something tells me that's a bit of a stretch. And it's time that I stop being so stubborn. So, I'm willing to compromise a bit." She leaned up against the counter while she sipped her tea. She could feel his intense stare and felt her body reacting again. "I think I should go take a shower and then pack a few necessities for my trip uptown."

When she left the room, Hunter texted Ryan to let him know he had the next couple days to install the security system. He fully expected Ryan to add his usual sarcasm but only got an "ok", which instantly put him on alert. Either Ryan was knee-deep in the investigation or he had uncovered something he wasn't ready to divulge.

Emma packed the necessities, although she wasn't completely sure what those were given this situation. She guessed it was a little bit of every-thing—casual, dinner-worthy, lounging. Once she was showered and her bag was packed, she walked into the kitchen to find Hunter deep in thought. She stared at him for a few seconds, not wanting to disturb whatever it was that was going on in his head. Over the past few days, she had found herself wondering what really made him tick. He really didn't seem like his father, who had been driven solely by power and money. Yet her research on Hunter a few weeks ago had revealed that Hunter was on the Forbes Top 50 list—an accomplishment his father never had achieved. She couldn't deny that he had drive and ambition, but he also had a softer side.

She knew Hunter had only become involved in the family business because of his father's untimely death. Prior to that, from the various newspaper articles, he seemed to have no interest. And even after his father's accident, it was another full year before he took complete control of the company due to the corporate bylaws that had been put in place. Hunter's father had added a contingency in case of his accidental death - Hunter would become interim CEO for six months and then after another six months would take official control of the company.

As Emma remembered this tidbit of information, something in the back of her mind was tingling. Something about this information seemed premeditated to her, especially given what had happened at her office. She tried to shake off the feeling that all of this was connected as she made her presence known to Hunter, who was still pondering life's wonders.

"Are you all packed?" was all Hunter said to Emma when she entered the kitchen.

"Um, yes, I think so. And it's not like I'm leaving the country. I can always come here to grab anything I forgot, I guess."

Hunter took Emma's bag and his laptop bag as he headed toward the door. She barely had time to put her shoes on before he was pressing the elevator button. Emma quickly grabbed her purse, made sure her door was securely locked, and met Hunter at the waiting elevator. They rode down to the lobby in silence, barely looking at one another. Emma could tell Hunter was on edge, which in turn, made her anxiety level off the charts.

The car was waiting for them as they stepped off the elevator. Both security guards nodded as they walked toward the door. Emma couldn't remember ever having seen security guards at the desk before. She surmised that Hunter must have added extra guards as a precaution, which didn't make her feel better.

CHAPTER 19

———

As they drove to Hunter's penthouse, Emma considered the last time she had been there and how much had happened since. When they arrived, they again rode the elevator in silence. The elevator doors silently slid open to reveal Ryan standing in the hallway. Emma wasn't sure if that was a good thing or not.

"Emma, how are you doing, darlin'? I'm sorry that we had to uproot you for a few days." It was strange to Emma how at-ease she felt with Ryan. He was obviously a man of mystery, but somehow, she knew he would do whatever he could to keep her out of harm's way.

"I'm better now that I've seen your chipper face." Emma flashed him a smile that said she was both fine and terrified at the same time.

"That's what I like to hear!" Ryan startled Emma by pulling her into a bear hug until she thought he was going to crack a few ribs. For the first time, Emma could confirm that Ryan was rock solid muscle. This was a man that definitely spent more than enough time working out. Emma figured he had more than his share of women throwing themselves at him. When Ryan finally ended the embrace, he gave Hunter a quick smirk. Hunter shook his head and brought Emma's bag to the guest room.

"You love to needle him, don't you?" Emma said slyly.

"You betcha! Keeps him on his toes. Look, go get settled in and then we'll all have a little family chat."

Emma eyed Ryan suspiciously as she headed toward the guest room. When she stopped in the doorway, she found Hunter unpacking her bag and putting everything in its place. "Thanks. I could have done that later."

"We are a full-service establishment, Ms. Sharpeton. And you deserve a little pampering. I'll be in the living room with Ryan. Join us when you're ready." With that, Hunter left the room and headed to the living room to join Ryan.

All Emma could do was sigh. This was overwhelming to say the least. She took a few minutes to look around the room. It was the same style as Hunter's bedroom with very similar furnishings and accents. The bathroom was white marble with a large stand-up glass enclosed shower and separate soaking tub. The walk-in closet had ample hanger space plus drawers and shoe racks. She could tell the bed was going to be heaven before she even sat down. As she sat on the bed to catch her breath, she heard whispering from the living room. Emma wasn't sure she even wanted to know what Ryan had uncovered but also knew that someone was playing roulette with her life, and she had to know why.

As Emma walked towards them, the men's conversation quieted. "No need to stop on my account, boys," she said as she entered the living room. Both men, who were standing next to the windows, turned to look at her simultaneously.

"Emma, let's sit down and I'll tell you what I've discovered so far." Ryan ushered her to the couch. The same couch she and Hunter had previously sat on not that long ago. Emma did as she was told as she looked at both of them. Hunter and Ryan each took one of the matching armchairs that faced the couch. Once the three of them were comfortable, Ryan leaned forward, "Did you know that your father used to work for Hunter's father?"

Emma was dumbfounded. She knew that her father was a chemist and had worked for a pharmaceutical company but had no idea it was for Philip Logan.

"I'll take your reaction to mean that you didn't know. Here's what I know—and it may not even be related. From what I can tell, your dad was working on a top-secret project involving a cancer drug."

Emma interjected, "I know that pharmaceuticals are very competitive, but it's not like there aren't other cancer drugs on the market."

"I know. That's what I was thinking, so I did more digging via some unorthodox methods. Logan Pharmaceutical wasn't trying to develop a drug to help manage a patient's cancer—they were trying to create the cure for cancer and a way to prevent it altogether. From what I can tell, they were extremely close." Ryan paused to gauge the reaction of his audience before continuing. "This cancer cure drug was from a plant extract—a plant that looks like had never been catalogued before. That's what Hunter's father was doing in the Amazon when he died."

"Even though this is interesting and a bit perplexing, I'm still not sure how my father fits into this or what is has to do with what's happening now." Emma was thoroughly confused and not sure how to process Ryan's information.

"I get it. And as I said before, it may have nothing at all to do with what's happening now. I just don't like coincidences unless they can be explained. And right now, this one is still a mystery. Do you remember your father ever talking about his work?"

"Sometimes, but most of the time he kept quiet about it. He always said that he'd bore us to death talking about his chemical analysis and formulas. We all used to laugh and then go on to other topics.

I still don't know what this has to do with anything," Emma replied with a gentle headshake.

Ryan knew that he had to proceed cautiously. There were more questions than answers and he didn't want to stir up a hornet's nest if he didn't have to. "Based on the research reports I was able to dig up, and don't ask me how please, Philip literally fell onto this unidentified plant while traipsing through the jungle. According to the notes we found, it had the most brilliant pink hues he had ever seen. When he couldn't find it in any plant classification database, he decided to have the sample analyzed. One thing Philip did was to document every step of the process so there was no mistake he was the perceived owner of this potential find."

Ryan paused to make sure he hadn't lost anyone before he continued, looking directly at Emma. "When Philip got back to the U.S., he hired your father. Apparently, your father was somewhat of a rock star when it came to developing medicinal plant extracts. I won't try to go into the details as half of them are way above my head." Emma and Hunter were both entranced listening to Ryan. "Craig Sharpeton spent the next year doing whatever it is that chemists do. And just before his death, he had a breakthrough. We were able to unencrypt a lot of the research but there are holes we're still working on. I'm not sure if these holes are intentional in case this ended up in a competitor's hands or if the research was never completed." Ryan paused.

"Emma, your dad was able to put most of the puzzle pieces together it seems. He discovered that a combination of the plant's root and flower created healing powers no one had discovered before. There were trials done with mice that produced some success, but he had yet to figure out the missing links. Or at least there isn't any documentation saying he finished the work." Ryan knew that Emma had a lot to absorb in a short amount of time. He needed to be patient with her and let her digest this at her own pace.

Emma sat quietly on the couch as Hunter moved from the chair to be next to her. She wasn't sure what she was supposed to do after learning all this about her father. Her heart ached with regret that she hadn't tried to learn more about her father's work and his life. She wondered if her mother knew any of this or if she was also in the dark.

Emma spoke evenly, "I remember that my father had a picture of this vividly pink plant hanging in his home office. I always thought it was the most beautiful thing I had ever seen. He would tell me that it paled in comparison to me, which always made me giggle. I actually still have the picture. Up until about two weeks ago, it was hanging in my work office. I decided to take it home to have it reframed—it's in my home office closet."

The world seemed to stop as all three connected yet another coincidence to this bizarre state of affairs. Ryan was the first to speak, "Another coincidence. Your office gets broken into and torn apart around the same time you bring the picture home."

Hunter, who had remained uncharacteristically quiet throughout the story-hour finally spoke, "It might be just a coincidence. And I know how you feel about coincidences, but what good is a picture of a plant when obviously my father had the almost completed formula?"

"I know. Like I said—more questions than answers. It's a tangled web. Every time I get any traction, it seems like I'm sucked into more questions. There's a bit more, so bear with me." Both Emma and Hunter nodded. "Two weeks after Emma's father's car accident, Philip boarded a plane back to the Amazon. He had already made several more trips there, all to the same location, before his own untimely demise. Since these were all private flights and not commercial, there isn't a lot of information, except the flight plans and customs receipts. Considering Philip's resources, I haven't been able to verify these aren't fraudulent."

Hunter piped up. "What did the customs receipts say?"

"All they said was that it was plant or vegetation material weighing less than fifty pounds. But he was able to bypass the required quarantine protocols, which leads me to believe he had inside help at the U.S. Customs and Border Protection's agriculture division. So, it doesn't take a brain surgeon to figure out he was bringing back more plants to continue with his little project. The trail goes cold after his death, which leads me to believe that he never completed the work that both he and Mr. Sharpeton had started. My guess is you would have heard something by now, Hunter, if anyone was working on this."

Hunter put his hands on his head as if trying to remember every conversation after his father's death. Something among all this non-information continued to nag at him. None of it made sense, and he still couldn't figure out what the intersection point was. Somehow, his family and Emma's had been linked more than tightly than he had ever realized. He couldn't help but think that maybe this was the reason his father had been so adamant he should not be involved with Emma.

"I never knew any of this. But then again, many of his special employees are no longer there. You know how he churned through people with his winning personality. I do know that he was passionate around cancer research as a result of losing his sister, my aunt. It was the one thing I ever saw him give a damn about besides himself. What little human emotion he had come out only when he talked about her."

"Okay, I think I've given you both some things to think about. I'll keep digging to see what else I can shake loose. Emma, hang in there, kiddo. You're in good hands here. I'll have your place all wired up in the next two days. You kids don't do anything I wouldn't." Ryan chuckled as he popped up out of the chair and headed toward the door.

Emma sprung up after him and surprised him with a hug as she whispered, "Thank you," in his ear. For a second Ryan blushed before he was tucked away in the elevator. Emma walked back into the living room to find Hunter standing at the window gazing at the city below them.

She tentatively joined him. "Penny for your thoughts."

He laughed. "Isn't that what I'm supposed to say to you? How are you holding up?"

"It's a lot to take in. I really wish I'd paid more attention to my father's work." Emma couldn't hide her regret.

"Don't start second-guessing yourself. I told you before, I was always jealous of the relationship you had with your father. He absolutely adored you, and you him. Cherish that." Hunter looked at Emma's big, green eyes. The next few days was going to be dangerous for both of them. Emotions were running higher than normal, and he knew he had to be the one who drew the line in the sand.

Hunter broke the silence. "What would you like to do this afternoon?"

"Doesn't matter to me. Anything is fine."

"How about we take a drive to Kennebunkport? There's a great restaurant there where we could get dinner."

"Sounds nice." Emma tried to sound convincing.

"Or we could just hang out here and watch movies or go to the driving range or the indoor pool. Completely up to you. I'll let you ponder that while I excuse myself to hit the loo."

Emma took the time to digest everything Ryan had said. She still couldn't fathom her father getting involved with Philip Logan. From a personality standpoint, they were on opposite ends of the spectrum. Craig Sharpeton was kind, the definition of integrity. Philip was a ruthless person who didn't believe in any sort of ethics.

She had known that her father had been sought after by many of the large research facilities, so it was plausible he was a 'rock star' as Ryan had put it. Emma didn't hear Hunter come back into the room. She stared out the window towards the harbor. One of the cruise ships was pulling out of port, heading to Bermuda for a week of fun in the sun. Everyone on board would be excited for their upcoming adventure. It reminded her of family cruises she had gone on a lifetime ago.

"It's pretty cool to see the cruise ships leaving port from up here," Hunter said, startling Emma.

"Yes, it is. They look so small." Emma looked at Hunter and smiled as she said, "Let's go to the driving range. It will do me some good to concentrate on something else."

"The driving range it is. Let me call ahead so it's all ready for us." Hunter went into his office and began to dial the phone. Emma wasn't sure what he meant by 'getting it ready' but guessed she'd soon find out. "It's all set. Let's have a light lunch and then we'll be on our way." Hunter scurried into the kitchen, began taking out dishes, and digging around in the fridge.

"Do you need any help?" Emma hollered into the kitchen.

"No, love, just relax. It will only take me a minute or two."

Emma smiled to herself. She had a feeling that Pauline had already left some prepared meals for Hunter in the refrigerator, and he was just putting it on plates. She approached the kitchen as Hunter placed two plates of Caesar salad on the bar.

"Lunch is served," he said as he took a bow.

Emma lightly clapped as she sat down on the bar stool. She watched Hunter intently as he poured a glass of chilled white wine and placed it in front of her. The universe seemed intent on bringing them closer together. Emma had a feeling that this situation wasn't done by a long shot—in fact, it had just begun.

They both aggressively dove into their salads in silence. Hunter startled Emma as he put his hand on top of hers. "We'll figure all this out. I promise." Once they had devoured their lunch, he cleared the dishes away. On his way to the sink, he stole a glance of Emma. Her eyes glistened with tears. He knew he needed to give her time to process all these events, so he turned away to pretend he was still cleaning up the kitchen.

CHAPTER 20

———

E mma quietly walked back into the living room to the panoramic windows and stared out at the waterfront as U2's *Every Breaking Wave* softly filled the room on the Bose surround sound. She hadn't even realized that Hunter had come into the room until he slid his arms around her shoulders. She leaned back into his chest and let him engulf her with his strength.

Hunter who broke the silence, "I am truly sorry that you have to go through all of this, kitten."

"I know you are." Emma straightened up. "Let's go to the driving range so I can kick your butt. And I'm an Aries with a mean competitive streak." Without hesitation, she turned and kissed him on the lips then darted down the hall to her room.

Emma couldn't believe she had just done that. She was spiraling out of control when it came to Hunter. As she was scolding herself, she heard the door to the bedroom open. She turned to find Hunter leaning against the door with a mischievous smile. Emma's heart began to palpitate so hard she thought she was going to faint. Neither of them took their eyes off each other as Hunter sauntered over to Emma.

"I know that I said we should wait until after the gala to see where this was heading, but I can't take this anymore! I don't just want you—I *need* you. And I need you now. We both need a break from reality—even if it's just for a little bit."

Hunter stroked Emma's cheek, looking deeply into her eyes, while his other hand traveled down Emma's back to her buttocks. Emma's breathing slowed as she savored the feeling of his hands on her. She was mesmerized as he lightly kissed her neck, making her body tingle.

Emma placed her hands on his chest, feeling every contour. His breathing quickened the minute she touched him. Everything seemed to be in slow motion, emphasizing every breath and touch between them. As Hunter took off Emma's sweater and pants with expert efficiency, he marveled at her sculpted body, all her curves waiting for his exploration. She was exquisite and she was his, at least for today, he thought.

Hunter gently guided Emma backwards to the king size bed as he shed his shirt. Emma unbuckled his belt and then his pants to reveal his enthusiasm. As Hunter stepped out of his pants, he moved Emma further up on the bed.

With one quick motion, he unclasped her lace bra to reveal yet another beautiful sight. He let his fingers caress her smooth skin, teasing her only enough for her to catch her breath. Hunter gracefully moved like a snake up her body, so he was perfectly positioned for his tongue to take over where his fingers left off.

Emma gasped as his tongue danced on her breasts, which were swollen with anticipation. He was the hunter and she was his prey, and for the first time, she realized she didn't mind at all. He ran his fingers down the front of her body giving her goose bumps until he reached his destination. He took his time making sure that every inch was thoroughly explored and circled back multiple times. When he felt that Emma was just about to dive off the cliff, he began his deep exploration to the sound of her moaning. They were instantly in a rhythm that was like a favorite song neither wanted to end until they both cried out simultaneously as *Return to Innocence* flowed from the living room.

Neither Emma nor Hunter wanted to move or break the bond between them. Emma was the first to move, to Hunter's disappointment. She slowly slipped herself off of Hunter to retreat to the bathroom. Panic filled Hunter that he did something wrong until she sauntered back to the bed, still gloriously naked, and slipped up his body like he had done with her moments before.

In a sultry voice she said, "Remember how we used to go horseback riding when we were kids?" Hunter nodded, not exactly sure where this was heading, just as she began her own exploration, her stroking causing him to gasp. "Riding was always so sensual. Every part of our bodies in rhythm." She gazed at Hunter as she continued with her mission. "Ah, I see you remember. Very good."

Without another word she positioned herself on top of him and enveloped him inside her. For the first time in days, she was in absolute control and her confidence radiated. She slowly moved up and down teasing him with every movement. None of the events from the last several days were able to infiltrate into these moments. This was a haven for them as both, once again, simultaneously reached their destination.

"Obviously we must have gone to the British version of a driving range." Emma couldn't help herself. They both burst into laughter as Hunter drew Emma closer to him and held her.

"And you still got to kick my butt as you so eloquently put it earlier."

"So true. Who says golf can't be invigorating?"

They stayed in each other's arms for what seemed like an eternity until reality made its cruel entrance once again with the sound of Hunter's phone. Hunter ignored it and wrapped his arms tighter around Emma willing the world to go away for a few more minutes. His phone rang again, and Hunter knew that he had to answer it as a sense of dread washed over him.

Hunter slid out of Emma's embrace and, still naked, walked to the kitchen where he left his phone. Emma couldn't quite make out the conversation but knew in her heart that they had just gotten back on the roller coaster ride of the last several days. When Hunter returned, he put the phone on the nightstand and engulfed Emma with his body once again.

Emma was the first to break the silence. "Are you going to tell me about the call?"

Hunter sighed. "Sorry. I'm still trying to make sense of everything in my head." He paused and Emma could see he was shaken up. "Emma, how well do you know your assistant's boyfriend?"

"Um, not at all. She tends to have a flavor of the month and as soon as I learn their name, she's on to the next Mr. Right. Why?"

"This is just preliminary so you cannot say anything to anyone. Got it?" He paused, waiting for her response. "Emma?"

"Yes! Got it. Now what the fuck is going on? You're starting to scare me." Emma trembled.

Hunter could see the panic in her eyes and knew he had to position this right the first time or it would be like a volcano erupting. "As I said, preliminary, non-confirmed reports are looking like her 'flavor of the month' may have had something to do with the break-in at your office." Emma began to say something, but Hunter cut her off. "He fits the general description and the police were able to lift one print that didn't belong to anyone on your staff or the cleaning crew."

"That's not really a lot of evidence. The description probably fits half the guys in the city. And he could've picked her up for lunch one day or something like that and left the fingerprint."

"Emma, you're not understanding. The print was left in *your* office, on the corner of *your* desk. It is completely out of place. And there was a trace of red paint with the print." Hunter took a deep breath before continuing. "And there's something else. Remember last night when you were mad at me and stormed down the street toward your condo? You literally ran into a guy walking the opposite direction. Do you remember?"

Emma nodded but said nothing as Hunter continued, "Well, Ryan was able to work his computer magic and it looks like the guy who broke in and this guy are the same person."

"How can you tell? No one could see his face on the security camera." Emma's confusion could clearly be detected in her tone.

"I don't know. It's some sort of recognition software that only needs certain data points or something. Anyway, Ryan ran the program three times and got the same result. They are the same person. And we think that person is also your assistant's boyfriend."

The walls seemed to be closing in around Emma and she desperately needed air. She sprinted from the bed and opened the glass door to the wrap-around deck. Emma couldn't articulate what she was feeling: scared, angry, violated, vengeful, sad, all of the above. Hunter watched Emma breathe in the fresh air as if she couldn't get enough. He was as lost as she was in all this, not understanding what the end game was.

"Although I don't mind you being an exhibition-ist, it may not be the best time to show all of Boston your prize possessions."

Emma hadn't realized that she was still naked and didn't care. Someone was coming after her whether she had something on or not. The anger started consuming her as she turned to Hunter with fire in her eyes. Hunter didn't like the emotional direction this was heading and wasn't quite sure what to do to keep her calm.

"Hunter, don't look at me like I'm a wounded bird. You know me better than that! This is over-whelming and yes, I'm full of so many different emo-tions right now. The one at the top of the list at this specific moment is rage. I won't do anything stupid but just know that I will not stand by and let this ass-wipe take any more from me than he already has!"

Tracey L. Ryan

With that declaration, she strode into the bathroom and closed the door so hard that the Tiffany lamps on the nightstands trembled. Hunter could hear the shower come on as he closed the balcony door. Today had been about impulses, and he wasn't about to stop as he opened the bathroom door.

Steam had quickly taken over the room, and he could see her silhouette in the glass shower. When he opened the shower door, steam escaped to reveal Emma lathering gel across her erogenous body. "I'm not going to let him take anything else from you. And I'm sure as bloody hell not going to let him come between us." And for the next twenty minutes, no one else existed.

CHAPTER 21

———

That night, Emma slept in Hunter's bed for the first time. Both were exhausted from the events of the day and were content just holding each other. Hunter dozed off quickly while it took longer for Emma to calm her thoughts. When she finally slipped into slumber, her dreams took over. She was standing in the middle of a dark room with the only light being a spotlight that shined on her. People formed a circle around her, and they were pointing and laughing at her. At first, she didn't understand until she looked down to see that she was completely naked. She desperately tried to cover herself when two people from the darkness came out and each grabbed one of her arms to stop her from covering up. She had the feeling that she knew them, but couldn't place them in her mind.

After the men restrained her, the leader came from behind the shadows and instructed someone to go get the supplies. Emma couldn't comprehend

Tracey L. Ryan

what was happening. Even after she saw the leader, she still didn't understand. When he came closer to her she started to squirm. The other man came into the light and Emma could tell that it was the man from the street outside her apartment building. "Why are you doing this to me?" she asked the man.

It was the leader who spoke and only said one word: "Whore." Then the man from the street proceeded to write the word 'whore' all over Emma's body with red paint and his fingers. There wasn't a spot that he didn't touch as the others looked on. Emma was humiliated but even worse, she was aroused, and the man knew it. He leaned and whispered, "Now that's being a good little whore." Then he and the others walked away leaving her alone.

"Emma. Emma, wake up! You're having a nightmare." Hunter shook Emma, trying to wake her from her nightmare. Slowly her eyes opened. She was momentarily disoriented.

"Emma, you're with me. You're safe. Jeez, what the bloody hell were you dreaming about?"

"I...I...I'm not exactly sure. I think the man from the street was there and red paint." Emma sat up, trying to get her bearings and calm herself down. She wasn't about to tell Hunter the details of this nightmare, especially when she didn't understand it herself. "I'm fine. You know how sometimes your subconscious just doesn't let go. Sorry I scared you."

Hunter pulled Emma back under the covers and wrapped his body around hers. "You never have to apologize for anything you do." And with that, they both tried to salvage what they could for sleep before the early morning sun washed over them.

Hunter woke up to Emma looking at him intently.

"Morning, kitten. Did you sleep okay the rest of the night?"

"Yes. Sorry again for waking you. I have an idea how I can make it up to you."

"Now I am very awake and curious." Hunter propped himself up on his elbow, smiling at Emma quizzically.

"Well, then, Mr. Curious, leave it to me." Emma hopped out of bed and hurried down the hall toward the kitchen. Hunter heard lots of clanking and rattling and decided to stay where he was until it calmed down. When the noise settled, he started to smell the aromas of a fine English breakfast.

Hunter padded down the hall to find Emma with only an apron on and her backside saying 'good morning' to him. Emma spun around and gave him a disapproving look. "Go back to bed. Your breakfast will be served to you momentarily." She turned back around to tend to the eggs and bacon in the frying pans. Hunter admired her assets for a few minutes longer before he did as he was told.

Just as he positioned himself back in bed, Emma entered with a tray full of nourishment for both to enjoy. She placed the tray on his lap and then with one quick motion untied her apron as she slid back into bed. When they were both done enjoying Sunday breakfast, Hunter placed the tray on the nightstand and began to show his appreciation just as his phone vibrated.

"What?" Hunter shouted into the phone.

"Good morning, darling. Did I wake you?" The woman on the other end really didn't care if she woke Hunter.

"Morning, Mother. No, you didn't wake me. I was actually just about to insert myself into an important task. What can I do for you?" Hunter was pleasant but somewhat cool towards his mother, Emma noticed. She had always thought they were close but maybe things changed when his father died.

"I'm pulling up in front of your building now and thought we could have Sunday brunch together," Katherine Logan said with a hint of authority.

"Now is not a good time, Mother. I really wish you had called first." Hunter didn't try to hide his annoyance with the pending intrusion.

"I am calling first. Now drop whatever it is your doing and be ready to receive me in ten minutes." Katherine disconnected the phone as her driver pulled up in front of Hunter's building.

"Bloody fuck! My mother is on her way up here. Go get dressed." Hunter didn't wait for Emma to answer as he headed toward the shower.

Emma was a bit shocked as she headed to her own bathroom. She hadn't ever thought that she might have to see Hunter's mother again, let alone today. This was not helping her stress level as she took the quickest shower of her life.

By the time Emma came into the living room, mother and son were involved in an intense conversation that she wasn't sure she was supposed to be part of. Katherine was the first to notice Emma and quickly stopped the conversation.

"Good morning, Mrs. Logan." Emma tried to sound unaffected by the other woman's presence.

"Good morning, Emma. Hunter just told me about your rekindled friendship and that you are staying here for a couple of days. How nice to see you again," Katherine said with the hint of distain. "I didn't realize that you both already had breakfast. I never get to see my son these days and wondered if he was still alive since he never calls me. So, I figured that, per the usual, I would have to come see him."

"I wouldn't want to intrude on any quality mother-son time," Emma dished right back. "I actually have some work to catch-up on for the gala. Hunter, I'll be in your office if you need me." Emma smiled. Before she turned down the hall trying not to run, she looked back to Katherine. "It was nice to see you again."

Emma closed the door to Hunter's office partly because she wanted to be respectful of Hunter's privacy and so she couldn't get sucked into whatever drama was between Hunter and Katherine. She had never really known Hunter's mother while they were growing up. Katherine seemed pleasant enough back then, although Emma couldn't remember a single time that they ever had a real conversation. It was always limited to pleasantries like "hello" or "goodbye".

This gave her some time to herself to think. This weekend had been a blur and nothing was making sense. To Ryan's point, there were too many coincidences that just begged more questions. Then it hit her like a brick: her father had a home office at their house in Hardwicke. What if there were answers there? She used Hunter's landline to call her mother.

"Hello?" Victoria answered tentatively as she didn't recognize the number.

"Hi, Mom. It's me. I'm calling from Hunter's penthouse." As soon as the words came out of her mouth, she knew she was going to regret it.

"Hunter? As in Hunter Logan? So that is who you've been spending all your time with these days. Be careful, honey. Dating a man like that is like dancing with fire…you'll get burned at some point. It may be exciting to start out but a disaster in the end." There was genuine concern in Victoria's voice.

"Gee, thanks, Mom. Look, I didn't call to talk

about Hunter. Did you ever clean out Dad's office at the house?"

"I haven't had a chance the last couple times I was out to visit. Why?" Victoria's curiosity was piqued.

"Oh, nothing really. I was going to maybe take a ride out there today and finally start cleaning out the house." Emma tried to be casual so her mother wouldn't be alerted to her real agenda.

"That would be wonderful, especially since I've been begging you to do it for several months now. I really want to put it on the market since neither of us has a use for it now. Your dad would want that, too." Victoria was secretly relieved that she wouldn't need to clean out her late-husband's office. It was always his personal space and she knew that the pain of losing him would resurface as soon as she walked in that room.

"I know he would. It is just sad to see a chapter of our lives coming to a close. I think that's why I've been putting it off."

"Why the interest in his office?" Victoria was still confused why Emma would want to start with the office.

"Is there any paperwork or anything that I should save? Maybe Dad brought some work home that I should send to whatever company he was working for." Emma tried to play it cool with her mother as she didn't want to raise any suspicions.

"I'm sure you can toss all of it. His employer never asked us for anything after he died. Honestly, I can't even remember his boss's name. It was Baxter or something like that. I think he was based in South America or something. I guess I didn't pay much attention. Your father kept food on the table and a nice roof over our heads. I didn't need to know how he did it."

Emma realized that her mother didn't really know any more than she did about what her father had done for a living. All Emma could think was that this was like something out of a James Bond movie. "Okay, Mom. I'll see if I can make a dent in the clean-out today. I'll let you know if I find anything interesting. Take care of yourself. I love you."

"I love you, too." Both women disconnected the phone to retreat back to their own lives.

At that moment, there was a soft knock on the door as Hunter popped his head inside. "She left so it's safe for you to come out. And thanks a lot for leaving me in the dust. You were not playing fair at all," Hunter said with a playful smile.

"It sounded like you two needed some quality time together. You can thank me later. Not to change the subject, but I just called my mother."

"What is this? The day for motherly love?"

"Hush. My mother is nice. Yours is a force to be reckoned with. I gently prodded to see if my mom knew anything at all about my father's work. She knows about as much as I do, which isn't really anything. So, I have an idea if you are feeling adventurous."

Hunter braced himself.

"What if we take a ride to my house in Hardwicke today? My father kept a home office there and maybe there are some clues there. Couldn't hurt and ya never know…" Emma wasn't sure what Hunter's reaction was going to be as she patiently waited for his response.

"It might be good to get out of the city for a few hours. And a drive to the country could do us both some good. I just want you to prepare yourself in case we don't find anything."

"I know that. I promised my mother I'd start cleaning out the house so she can put it on the market and, to be honest, I have been procrastinating. So, this will kill two birds with one stone as they say. Thank you."

"No need to thank me. Where you go, I go. It's that simple." Hunter kissed her cheek and gave her a hug before returning to the bedroom to clear the breakfast dishes away.

CHAPTER 22

———

L eaving the city limits was like going from night to day. The traffic was all but non-existent; trees were budding; and the air felt cleaner and crisper. The two drove in silence, yet it wasn't an awkward silence. They were completely comfortable with taking in the scenery as they traveled back in time. Hunter pushed the silver metallic Porsche Panamera Turbo S on the winding country roads. Emma looked at him as a grin consumed him, making him look like the teenager she once knew in this quaint town.

Emma began gripping the armrest more tightly as Hunter continued to push the Porsche on the desolate road. "Ummm, this new car of yours seems to handle well." She hoped he would get the hint that they didn't need to drive like they were on a racetrack.

Instead, Hunter took this as Emma was showing genuine interest in what, he felt, was a magnificent piece of engineering. "Glad you like it! It can go 0-60 MPH in six seconds thanks to the V6 engine and 310 horsepower. It's incredible what they can build these days!" Hunter said, keeping laser focused on the road. The last thing he needed was for a deer to run out in front of them.

"I really am glad you like the car but how about we take it down a notch so we can enjoy the drive at a little less than the speed of light." Emma tried to sound calm and smile while she was still grasping the door handle.

Hunter slowed down to a reasonable speed for the remaining fifteen minutes of their ride with a twinge of disappointment. With speed no longer a factor, Hunter was able to sneak a peek at Emma while she gazed out the passenger window. The sunlight glistened on her honey blonde hair as it surrounded her in a warm glow. She looked almost angelic, he thought. He knew in the deepest depth of his soul that he would do anything to protect this angel.

Hunter slowed the car even more as they came over the knoll into the center of Hardwicke. He noticed how little the quaint country town had changed since he had last been there all those years ago. The town's common with its marble fountain, green grass, and park benches still defined tranquility. The various buildings surrounding the common were still grounded in history from over 250 years ago. He could remember the little country fair that happened every summer and eating chocolate ice cream on the porch of the general store. The nostalgia started to fog his instincts, but Hunter knew he needed to be sharp as a knife since no one knew where threats might come from. They could even be hidden in this picturesque, sleepy little town.

Hunter noticed a single tear silently slide down Emma's face. "How are you doing, Em?"

Emma wiped the tear away, "Ya, I'm okay. Just a little strange being back here since my father's death. It brought me back to the day of the funeral. There were cars parked everywhere in the center of town. Everyone came to honor a great man who died too soon. It all feels surreal right this minute."

Hunter could feel his own sadness creeping in—Craig had been the father he wished he had instead of his own. He had never told Emma, but he had attended her father's funeral, paying his respects from afar. "You know we don't need to do this. We can turn around and head back if you want to. You're the boss today."

"*Hmmm,* the boss, huh? All this power may go to my head." Emma looked thoughtfully at Hunter and managed a smile. "Thanks, but I actually need to do this…and I'm glad that you're here with me. It helps." She reached over and squeezed his hand, which was firmly attached to the stick shift.

Hunter pulled into the driveway of Emma's family home and cut the engine. Both sat in the car for a few minutes before Hunter made the first move. He gallantly opened the door for Emma while extending his hand to help her out of this very low vehicle, and gently kissed her lips.

"Don't get any ideas! We have work to do." Emma sidestepped him and ran to the front door with the key in her hand. Hunter was beside her in a matter of seconds as she was unlocked the door and disarmed the alarm system. Emma wrinkled up her nose at the stale air inside the house. She expected to smell the fruits of her mother's labor in the kitchen or fresh flowers from the garden in every room—not dust and musty air.

Hunter could tell she was taken back, "How about we open a couple windows to circulate the air in here? Then it won't feel so sterile."

"Probably a good idea. It seems so strange to be here without my father, or mother for that matter. I know that I should be over it by now but..." Emma's voice trailed off as she just stared into the empty kitchen.

"Everyone heals at a different rate, love. There aren't any set timetables and the hell with what others think." Hunter unlocked and opened the window over the kitchen sink to let the fresh air permeate through the space.

Emma started going from room to room, reacquainting herself with her childhood home. This was more than a house; it was a part of her and it felt as sad as she did at that moment. As she entered the living room, she smiled to herself as she looked at the red brick fireplace. Emma remembered one Christmas morning when she was about five years old. Her father had taken his winter boots, dunked them in the ash in the fireplace, and walked them across the floor to the Christmas tree so it looked like Santa Claus had delivered the presents. Her parents hadn't gotten the reaction they had hoped for. Instead, Emma had been furious at Santa for making such a mess.

"Penny for your thoughts," Hunter said as he looked intently at Emma's smile.

"Just remembering." Emma relaxed.

"Looks like it was a good memory." Hunter didn't want to pry into Emma's private thoughts.

"It was. It's amazing how many memories can be held in four walls and a roof." Emma sighed lightly. She knew she was procrastinating. "Come on. Let's do what we came here to do."

"We don't need to rush. It's fine if you want to get wrapped up in nostalgia. You look so at peace here. I wish I could give that to you."

Emma turned to see Hunter solemnly looking at her. She knew that being back in Hardwicke didn't have the same appeal for him. This was a magical place to Emma—one where dreams came true and love was overflowing.

"There will be time for nostalgia later. Let's go

sift through my father's office and see if we can start to unravel this mess." Before Hunter could respond, Emma was already halfway to her father's office, which was adjacent to the kitchen.

Emma started to remove all the sheets covering the furniture and filing cabinets. As she did so, a dust cloud that could rival a desert sandstorm took over the room, causing Emma to have a coughing fit. Hunter pushed passed Emma to open the only window in the small office and turn on the ceiling fan, hoping to make the air breathable again.

"Holy crap! Who would have thought so much dust could build up in a couple years? Good grief," Emma managed to sputter out. "I wonder if my mother left the old vacuum cleaner here. Would you be a dear and go look in the hall closet for me?"

Hunter bowed and took his leave to fulfill the task given to him. Emma continued to remove the sheets. She could hear Hunter cursing in the hallway closet. Who knows what her mother left in there? Emma thought as she shook her head. Within a few minutes she could hear the vacuum wheels running over the tile floor in the kitchen. Emma almost fell over when she turned to see Hunter maneuvering the machine like a pro. She couldn't suppress a little giggle.

Hunter didn't even notice Emma giggling as he worked his way around the office, even using the attachments to reach up to the corners to suck up the collection of cobwebs. Satisfied he had done the best job he could, he packed up the contraption perfectly and rolled it back to its hiding place. He swaggered back to the office with a look of satisfaction for conquering this domestic challenge. Emma couldn't help but be amused as she knew that domestic tasks were definitely not his specialty. Hunter smirked as he engulfed her in a hug that seemed to suspend time briefly.

"Come on, Mr. Domestic. We have work to do here." Emma grinned as she looked into his mysterious ice blue eyes. She wished she knew what he was thinking— not just about being back in this house, but the whole situation. Emma knew that Hunter was being evasive with her and, for now, she was content to pretend he didn't know any more than she did. Her biggest fear was that her father had somehow been caught up in all of this. No little princess wanted the image of her perfect father shattered.

Emma gently ran her hand over her father's antique roll-top desk. Another memory came rushing back to her: Sitting on her father's lap while he balanced the checkbook and did other paperwork. She had always been fascinated by the things that he did, even mundane chores. Her mother had left the office untouched after her father died. Everything was exactly the way that he had left it the night he was killed. This revelation sent a shiver up her spine and a sudden chill filled the air. Hunter saw the goosebumps on her arms and closed the window, thinking it was due to the breeze coming through. Emma smiled but didn't tell him it wasn't the breeze causing the sudden coldness.

"How about we divide and conquer? I'm not really sure what we're looking for so why don't you start with the file cabinet, and I'll start with the desk?" Emma asked Hunter.

"I'm not really sure what we're looking for, either. And this is all probably a long shot." Hunter moved over to the file cabinet and started at the top drawer while Emma sat in her father's chair at the desk. She pushed away any more memories as they weren't helping her with the here and now.

Emma opened the roll-top on the desk to reveal the familiar cubby holes where her father kept the bills and other household documents. There were file folders still sitting on the desktop with her father's handwriting all over them. It was the first time she had seen his handwriting since his passing and it felt like she was invading his privacy. Emma tried to control the emotions that were bubbling to the surface and about to explode.

She managed to compose herself and continued in her quest. The right top drawer produced the usual pens, pencils, calculator, scrap paper, paper clips, and spare keys. Again, a small wave of emotion ran over her as she realized that her father had been the last person to touch any of these things. Emma shook off the feeling and moved to the second drawer where she found pads of paper and unused notebooks. So far, just the typical desk-type stuff that anyone would keep.

The third drawer was all household files—old bills, bank statements, insurance information. Emma went through each file to make sure there wasn't anything of importance that might have been hidden in there. Nothing stood out, so she shifted to the left side of the desk. Again, the first two drawers were typical desk-type items. Emma sighed and wondered if Hunter was having better luck, although she didn't want to ask him. She knew that if he found anything, he would say something, or at least she hoped he would. For a brief instance, she wondered what secrets his family's country house held. She probably didn't want to know. There are some things that are better left alone—no need to disturb the rattlesnake.

The final drawer was more fruitful. There were many files that seemed related to her father's work life. Many of which she couldn't really make heads or tails of—hand-written notes with formulas, pictures of different plants, and some typed notes. Emma perused through the overstuffed files one by one. As she was reaching for the last file folder, her hand brushed against something taped to the bottom of the drawer above. Emma carefully pulled it free. In her hand was a flash drive.

As it rested in her hand, a thousand different thoughts raced through her head. What was on the drive? Why was it hidden? Did it have anything to do with her father's death? Or what was going on now? Could it just be something he didn't want her mother to see? The panic started infiltrating her normally logical brain before she snapped herself out of it.

She looked over her shoulder to see Hunter still rummaging through the file cabinet and separating files into different piles on the floor. "Hunter, I think I found something."

Hunter didn't look up from the task at hand, "What'd you find, love?"

"Did you bring your laptop by any chance?" Emma asked anxiously.

Hunter cursed to himself as he ended up with another paper cut from the file folders. "Sorry… what did you need?" He looked up to find Emma holding out the flash drive. "I've got my laptop in the car. I'll go grab it, and then you can tell me how you found this."

Hunter dashed out of the house to the car and was back in seconds. Emma noticed that when he came back into the office, carrying the laptop, he wasn't even out of breath, nor had a hair out of place. She really did wonder if he was super-human sometimes.

"Now, while I boot this thing up, tell me how

you found this." Emma noticed an edge to Hunter's voice like similar to the tone he'd had about the incident at her office. This was the cold and calculating side of him that she wasn't always fond of.

"I was going through the last drawer in the desk and the top of my hand brushed up against something that was taped to the bottom of the drawer above it. I pulled it free and this landed in my hand. Do you think it has anything to do with this whole mess?"

Hunter knew Emma was looking for reassurances that he couldn't provide. He couldn't help but think this was another piece of the puzzle. Emma handed the flash drive to Hunter and intently watched him as he slid it into the USB port. Both waited in silence for what seemed like an eternity and both were disappointed when they saw the username and password box appear on the screen.

"Well, it stands to reason that this would be password protected if your father was hiding it." Hunter popped out the drive from his laptop as neither of them would be able to get any further with opening it. "I can have Ryan take a look at it and see if he can find a way to crack the password. You didn't, by any chance, come across a listing of your father's usernames and passwords?" Hunter flashed a smile in Emma's direction although she was in deep thought. Hunter nuzzled up to Emma's neck to try to reassure her that they would figure all of this out, eventually.

"I didn't find his passwords, but I did find some files that could be important." Emma grabbed the handful of colorful folders from the desk and handed them to Hunter.

"These look like the same type of info that is in these folders over here from the cabinet and what Ryan had told us was in that encrypted email. I wonder why they weren't filed together?" Hunter pondered aloud. "Could be that he didn't have the chance to file them before the accident." Hunter winced as the words came out of his mouth.

"It's okay. I know what you meant. Really, I'm fine," Emma lied. She was anything but fine with this whole situation. As Emma flipped through some of the files Hunter had found, she noticed many were dated. "Do the files I gave you have dates on them?"

Hunter checked. As had been the case with the other files, those also had dates. Emma and Hunter began organizing the files in sequential order, hoping that it might tell them a story. Once the files were in sequential order, both of them sat on the floor and scanned through them one at a time. An hour went by as they finished with the last folder.

The files were setup as some sort of research journal - they had dated notes on different experiments and their corresponding results. Also included were different chemical formulas, which neither

Emma nor Hunter understood, and images of drawings with similar formulas. Hunter had never seen anything of this nature previously, regardless of his company's involvement in pharmaceutical research. He could see that Emma was as perplexed as he was.

"Your dad was a chemist, so it makes sense that he would have notes like this." Hunter scratched his chin before continuing, "I'm not exactly sure what it means or if it means anything. For all we know, it could be the formula to the next big thing in perfume."

Emma raised an eyebrow at Hunter to let him know that he was completely grasping at straws. "You and I both know that this isn't for perfume." She left it at that as she began to pull herself up off the floor and wiped any dust off herself. Emma was starting to feel uncomfortable again just as she heard the front door to the house open.

Hunter sprang to his feet and instinctively put himself in front of Emma as they slowly inched their way into the kitchen. They were greeted with a 9mm pistol pointed squarely at them. Once Hunter refocused his attention away from the barrel of the gun and to the person holding the weapon, he was able to breathe again. The 6'2" older man with a crew cut and about 200 pounds of lean muscle was the Hardwicke police chief.

"Good afternoon, Chief Dyson." Hunter addressed the man calmly and with respect as Emma peered around Hunter to verify who was in her house.

"Hunter Logan. Never expected to see you in these parts again. May I ask what you are doing inside the Sharpeton residence?" Chief Dyson was never one to mince words.

Emma stepped from behind Hunter and addressed the chief. "Hello, Chief. We didn't mean to startle the neighbors." She knew exactly who had called the police. It was the same nosy neighbors who used to call when Emma had parties whenever her parents were out of town.

"Emma! It has been a while since you've been back here. I think the last time was at your father's funeral. You look great! The city must be treating you well." The chief beamed at Emma as he holstered his weapon. Emma remembered the chief, only a patrolman in those days, stopping by for coffee while on duty and playing a few hands of Gin Rummy with his best friend, Craig.

The chief continued. "Yes, the neighbors did give me a call. They said they saw a strange car in the driveway and wanted to make sure no one was breaking in. Better safe than sorry. We've had a few break-ins lately, and I promised your mother I'd look after this place. How is she, by the way?"

"Oh, you know Mom. She's as crazy as ever. I'll tell her you were asking about her."

Tracey L. Ryan

"Please do. Well, sorry for intruding." As he turned to leave, the chief suggested that Emma call him the next time she's planning on visiting so that the cavalry didn't show up. Emma nodded in agreement as the chief headed back to his police cruiser parked out front.

"Well, that was interesting. And glad to see that you two still don't like each other."

"It's not a question of liking him. I think he's done a fine job managing to keep this little town safe. He and my father hated each other and that was mostly my father's fault. No one was going to tell Philip Logan that he had to stop at a stop sign or that he was speeding." Hunter shrugged and gathered up all the files so they could take them with them back to the city.

Emma took one more walk around the house to make sure that all the windows were closed and locked and the lights were shut off. She could still feel her father's presence and smiled again at all the happy memories this house held for her. Hunter was on his way out to the car as Emma had the sudden urge to check the basement. She unlocked the door and turned on the light as she peered down the stairs. She crept halfway down the stairs and looked around the musty, subterranean space.

This house was over 175 years old, and the basement was proof of that. Back in the 1800's, foundations were made from rocks and the gaps filled in with mud and dirt. The only natural light was from one small window that her father had installed years ago that was just above ground level. The once dirt floor had been covered over with cement years ago along with the gaps between the rocks. The ceiling still showed the bottom of the original hardwoods from the floor above and were a testament to the craftsmanship of that time period.

It looked like it had been years since someone had been down there, except for the population of spiders she knew were lurking in the dark shadows. Even the monstrous furnace wasn't as scary as it had been when she was a child. Her father's workbench was just as he had left it, along with shelves of paint and a variety of tools. She flashed back to when she as about 10-years-old and helping her father with one of his many projects around the house—she remembered how he always called her his assistant as he taught her which tools were needed for the job. Emma shook the memory out of her head. This was all her imagination given the stress of the last few days. She went back up to the kitchen, careful not to bump her head on the low stairway ceiling. Hunter was waiting patiently.

"Wasn't sure where you had disappeared to. Everything alright?" Hunter said as he watched Emma secure the padlock on the basement door.

"Everything's fine. I just wanted to check since we were here." Emma figured that Hunter would think she had completely lost her marbles if she told him how spooked she suddenly was in this house. Emma took one last look at her father's office before Hunter ushered her out the door.

CHAPTER 23

The ride back to the city was solemn as Emma stared out the window. They took a more scenic route than on the ride in, which led them past the entrance of the Logan family's estate. Emma noticed Hunter didn't slow down as they passed the stately elegant entrance with its dark wood privacy gate and multi-colored stone columns on either side that opened to a custom stone driveway. Emma knew that Philip hadn't put these up simply to display his wealth, but also for security. There were several well-hidden security cameras at the entrance and guests needed to use an intercom to call to the main house for admittance.

Emma had always thought it was a little magical when the gates opened to reveal the long winding driveway, which was lined with native hickory trees. On either side were grassy fields that had the most beautiful wildflowers in the spring. Emma had to hand it to Philip, he had spared no expense in designing this stylish country estate. It probably rivaled some English estates.

Emma noticed how tense Hunter got as he drove past the house and decided not to ask if he wanted to stop. Besides, they both needed time to reflect on their current state of affairs. Growing up, Emma had loved reading mysteries. In the summer, she would sometimes read two books in one weekend. She had never dreamed she'd be an unwilling participant in her own mystery.

It was dusk by the time they reached the city. Emma had fallen asleep on the ride. She woke, stretching with the grace of a feline as Hunter chuckled. "Good evening, kitten." Hunter's eyes seemed to light up the car when he used Emma's pet name from so long ago.

"Looks like we made good time getting back to the city. I don't even want to know how fast you were driving," Emma said sarcastically as she smiled.

Hunter eased the car into his designated parking spot in his building's private garage and turned off the engine. Emma had to admit that this was an exquisite car. Before she realized, Hunter was opening her door and helping her out of the vehicle.

"I know you really love the car—even if you won't admit it," Hunter said smugly as they walked to his private elevator. He held Emma's hand the short ride up to the penthouse. Very naughty thoughts were going through his head. He couldn't wait to get Emma undressed, maybe even in the foyer, as he smirked to himself.

Both were surprised when the doors opened, and they could hear voices coming from the living room. Hunter tensed and instinctively put Emma behind him for the second time that day as they slowly walked in to find Ryan and Katherine Logan laughing over a bottle of wine. Hunter managed to grunt, "Hello," and let go of Emma.

"Ryan. Mrs. Logan. What a surprise." Emma tried to sound gracious.

"Well, the surprise was all ours when we found you not at home and instead in Hardwicke," Katherine said with distain. It was no secret that Katherine had never liked the Hardwicke estate. She had never enjoyed the slow-paced country lifestyle and always favored the city life.

"How would you know where we were?" Hunter snapped.

"Calm down, mate. GPS in your car, remember? Had it installed not only so you wouldn't need to ask for directions but also a security measure." Ryan flashed a smile.

"*Why* on earth did you go to Hardwicke, darling?"

"Not that it is any of your business, *Mother*, but we decided to take a ride in the country and just ended up there. You know how beautiful it is this time of year." It was Hunter's turn to flash a smile.

Emma felt uneasy with the civilized sparring match happening in front of her. "I'm going to go take a quick shower." She exited quickly but not before Hunter grabbed her and kissed her. She was all for PDAs, but the situation seemed to be getting stranger by the minute.

As Emma closed the door to her bedroom, she could still hear the tenseness of the conversation between mother and son. Neither was backing down, and she knew that Hunter would be seething. Her guess was that the only reason he didn't throw out his mother was because Ryan was there. And if Ryan was there, he must have some information to report.

When Emma reappeared in the living room, fully clothed and with damp hair, she noticed they had one less guest. "Your mother left so soon?"

Hunter snorted as he took a large swallow of his Four Roses Small Batch Barrel Bourbon on the rocks. "She needed to go to some charity thing with her society friends. Something to do with saving the planet, I think. It's just up the block so she decided to do another surprise visit today." Hunter finished his glass and proceeded to pour another one, this time without the rocks.

Ryan sat in the leather chair, amused at what had happened over the last hour. "Emma, you are looking very refreshed after your afternoon in the country."

"Thanks, Ryan. Amazing what the fresh air will do for you. Now, can we dispense with all this nonsense and put our cards on the table?"

"Ah, a woman after my own heart. Hunter, you better keep a tight hold on this one. I may steal her right out from under you...*pun intended*." Ryan burst into one of his belly laughs that was contagious and soon the whole room was laughing. "Hunter gave me the supersonic version of what you found at your house, Emma. And again, we seem to have more questions than answers."

"How is my new-fangled alarm system coming? And my office?" Emma inquired.

"Both are great! We were able to completely restore your office to its original pristine look, so no one will be the wiser. And your apartment is yours...whenever you wish. I'll have to show you how to operate it - but other than that, you are good to go." Ryan was so proud of himself that he didn't notice the disappointment that briefly slide across Emma's face.

Emma quickly composed herself, "That's good. I don't know how to repay you." She gave Ryan a big hug and kiss on the cheek. Despite being sorry to end her time at Hunter's condo, she really was grateful.

"I can think of a few ways." Ryan glanced at Hunter before continuing. "We'll figure something out." Ryan chuckled.

Hunter rolled his eyes, "Can we get down to business?" The serious tone engulfed the room and sobered up the threesome. "Based on what we've found so far, this puzzle is getting more complex by the minute. What we do know is that there is a connection between the Sharpeton and Logan families. Why and what it means are still unknown."

Each of them silently reflected on all they had learned. Emma was the first to break the deep thoughts. "This is going to sound very geeky, but what if we went old school and wrote everything down on a whiteboard like they do on the cops shows? Then we could start to visually see gaps or connections."

Both men nodded.

"Hunter, what if we use the interactive whiteboard in your office? That way the data will be automatically transferred to our laptops, and we already know your office is secure. It will also make it easier for my team to dissect the data."

"Agreed. It's been a long couple of days - how about we table this until tomorrow? I've got some work to finish up before my morning meetings, and I'm sure Emma is anxious to get back to her place." Hunter glanced at Emma in time to see the confusion in her eyes. "Ryan, would you mind taking her home so you can show her how the new alarm works?"

Ryan tried not to show his own confusion—he knew from years of experience that once Hunter made up his mind there was no changing it. "No problem! Emma, we can leave whenever you are ready. Be prepared to be completely wowed with my expertise."

Emma played along. "I'm sure that you're a master of many things and look forward to learning more than I ever wanted to know." Emma provided the appropriate smile in Ryan's direction making sure that Hunter also saw.

She knew that she shouldn't feel hurt by Hunter's dismissal. It felt like two steps forward always ended up with three steps backwards where Hunter was concerned. And once again that little voice in her head was telling her to run for the hills while she still could. It seemed like they had done a world tour over the last few weeks, only to end up right back where they started. It was a dance that was both exhausting yet exhilarating at the same time.

Ryan and Emma arrived at her apartment twenty minutes later. Emma wasn't exactly sure what to expect and only hoped that it wasn't going to take an engineering degree to work the security system. As they retreated from the elevator, Ryan went through a metamorphosis into a giddy boy with a new toy.

"Emma, you are really going to love this! It is super cool and has all the latest technology. Plus, it is hack proof. The only way this won't work is if you don't use it." He shot a discerning look at Emma. "Okay, your front door here is wired from the inside and has motion sensors and cameras."

Emma suddenly became self-conscious as she looked around for the cameras and couldn't find any. Ryan chuckled, "Do you honestly think so little of me that the cameras would be noticeable? I'm eternally hurt." Ryan feigned a shocked look. "I'm actually not going to tell you where the cameras are because I truly don't want you constantly looking at them. Just know that there are cameras inside and outside your apartment."

Emma began to open her mouth at the mention of cameras inside her private space as Ryan jumped in. "They won't be on all the time—only when you turn them on. And they are only in the main living area. Not in the bathrooms or bedroom. I'm not a total perv!"

"I didn't think you were a perv, I swear!" Emma blushed a little. "Continue with the tour."

"I'm just razzing ya. Okay—go ahead and unlock the door." Emma did as she was told and walked into a very silent foyer. Ryan saw the puzzled look on her face. "This isn't like a standard alarm where it announces to the world that it is there. Think of this like a bank alarm—silent. You have forty-five seconds to enter the code on the keypad, which is cleverly hidden in your coat closet."

Emma opened the closet, suddenly feeling the pressure of the countdown. The panel looked like an electrical fuse box. Inside was a keypad with numbers and letters. She looked at Ryan as if to say, "Do you expect me to guess at the password?"

"The password is Hardwicke5641. You can change it later if you want to—just don't make it something that anyone with an internet connection can find out about you." Emma typed in the password and the red flashing light changed to solid green.

"That was easy enough. But my guess is there's a whole lot more to this thing than meets the eye." Emma winked at Ryan.

"You got it, like moi!" Ryan flashed a smile that Emma guessed made some women melt. "We won't go over every little detail tonight. I'll just give you the basics to get you started."

Emma let out a sigh of relief.

"Let's see, I told you about the cameras. You can put them on if you are here or if you are out of the apartment. Just press this button to turn them on." Ryan pointed to a button on the control panel with a camera icon. "Just remember that if you turn them on and you are home, don't walk around in the main living area naked. Well, you could, but then the boys downstairs monitoring would get all excited and it would just get messy."

"Got it—no being an exhibitionist."

"When you set the system when you leave, closing the front door will automatically turn on the motion sensors. Just let me know if you decide to get a cat or something as we'll need to adjust the sensors." Emma nodded. "As I said, the boys downstairs are monitoring 24/7 and a backup of the video and data is being sent to Hunter's office."

Ryan continued with the instructions. "The windows have sensors on them. If you unlock the window from the inside and open it, it will register on the system, but nothing will happen. If someone tries to open the window from the outside, it will immediately set the alarm off. And I know what you are going to say about being on the top floor. Someone could theoretically repel down from the roof if they really wanted to."

Ryan took a breath and resumed. "Here's where you can see if the alarm has been tripped. If you see these three lights flashing, get the hell out of the apartment ASAP—got it?"

"Got it! This is very sophisticated. I feel a bit foolish having all this security." Emma tensed slightly with the realization of why she would need the sophisticated security system.

"I'd rather you feel foolish than dead. I don't mean to scare you, but we have no clue what is going on, *and* Hunter would never forgive me if anything happened to you. The wrath of Hunter is not something I ever want to experience," Ryan said seriously.

"Ryan, thanks for everything. I truly mean it."

"No problem," Ryan started to leave but paused to say, "Look, I know that Hunter can be an ass sometimes. He really does care about you and this thing has him scared. Just don't take things like tonight to heart." Ryan kissed the top of Emma's head and disappeared into the elevator.

Emma didn't know if she was coming or going, but knew she needed to go to bed. She had a lot of work to do this week for the gala and needed to focus. She resigned herself to the fact that in order to get at least seven hours of sleep, she would need the help of a little blue pill. Emma hated taking medicine of any kind, but tonight she wanted to be comatose.

CHAPTER 24

A s Emma entered her office building on Monday morning, she felt refreshed for the first time in several weeks. Stan was on the phone when she came in but still managed to give her a big wave and a "Hello". Emma returned the gesture and headed up to her office. In the elevator, she realized that this would be her first time back since the incident on Friday night. A chill ran up her spine as images of that night replayed in her head.

When the elevator doors opened, she could hear the hustle and bustle of the office. It had a calming effect on her as it was a sign of normalcy. Ashley came charging around the corner from the kitchen trying to balance a cup of tea and walk in 4-inch spikes. "Morning, boss! I'll go put this in your office then grab my tablet so we can run through this week's priorities."

Emma tentatively walked into her office and was amazed. She made a mental note to do something to repay Ryan. He had managed to transform the ugliness from Friday night into an exact replica of her original office. Emma was stunned—even though it was the same, it felt clean and new and refreshing.

"Emma, are you okay? You have a strange look on your face. Kind of like you'd never seen this office before." Ashley sat down and looked at her tablet.

"Everything is good, Ash." As Emma took off her coat and got herself organized, she asked Ashley to rundown the highlights for this week. Once they were finished, Emma dove head-first into the day with their weekly team meeting, budget reviews, and creative briefs. There was only fourteen more days until the gala and things were coming together nicely. Emma was always proud of her team—they had tremendous talent and worked exceptionally hard. This gala was going to give them the recognition they deserved. She just hoped that nothing in her personal life would interfere with that.

Monday turned into Tuesday and Tuesday turned into Wednesday. Hunter texted Emma a few times to check-in but they hadn't seen each other since Sunday night. Emma decided it wasn't necessarily a bad idea to get some distance for a few days. They both could use a break from the emotional roller coaster neither seemed to be able to get off of.

In a spur of the moment decision on Thursday, she texted Morgan and Hannah to see if they were free for a quick dinner. Both were tied up with work but promised that they'd catch-up over the weekend. The women were more than curious about Emma's extracurricular activities with Hunter. That conversation would be best had over many watermelon martinis.

With now only a week left until the gala, Emma decided on Friday afternoon to go to Hunter's office to finalize the layout plans and tie up any loose ends. She elected not to call ahead, which could go either way where Hunter was concerned. It was a bit childish, but Emma didn't care. She knew she was using the gala as an excuse to try to see Hunter.

Emma was still amazed by Hunter's office building as the cab pulled up in front. After she paid the cab driver, she headed to the main entrance only to see Ryan standing in front of the revolving door. This couldn't be good, she thought. Emma walked purposefully. "Hi, Ryan. I had a break in my schedule today and wanted to finalize the layout for the gala."

"Hi, Emma. You probably should've called first. Hunter is occupied with an important client this afternoon." Ryan persuaded.

"No problem. I only want to scope out the lobby again and then I'll be on my way." Emma tried to sound as casual as she could even though her mind was racing. She didn't know Ryan that well, but something was off about his tone. She got the distinct feeling he was trying to get her out of there.

"Emma, I'm sorry if I seem abrupt, but Hunter will be bringing this very important client down here in a few minutes. It really isn't a good idea for you to be here. I'll get you a cab." Before Emma could even respond, Ryan was ushering her out the door and hailing a cab.

As the cab pulled up, Emma caught a glimpse of Hunter in the lobby. He was dressed to kill in a tailored dark suit with light blue shirt and pale pink tie. She could only imagine how his eyes glimmered until she saw his client. She was about as tall as Emma, very slender with long, straight, blonde hair. She, too, was stunningly dressed in a tailored navy pantsuit that showed just the right amount of cleavage. As Emma got into the cab, she was left with the memory of the blonde woman kissing Hunter in a more than business partners way. In the matter of a few seconds, Emma's heart was painfully ravaged.

Emma decided to grab her laptop and files from the office and work from home the rest of the day, given her current mood. There were no texts, emails, or calls from Hunter—which sent a very clear signal to Emma. Reality sometimes threw a curveball to make sure that everyone was paying attention, and Emma was definitely listening.

After she finished the few things she needed to get done before the weekend, she setup time on Sunday morning for brunch with her friends. Champagne in the morning always helps, she thought. Emma was surprisingly serene when her phone buzzed. It was one of the guys from the front desk. "I'm sorry to disturb you, Ms. Sharpeton. There is a delivery for you. Do you want me to bring it up to you?"

"Umm, sure. That's fine. Thanks." Emma disconnected and, for a brief second, thought it might be flowers from Hunter. She quickly scolded herself - he probably didn't even know she had been at his building earlier. The front door buzzer interrupted her discussion with herself.

"Here you go, Ms. Sharpeton. Have a good night."

Emma could barely get "Thanks" out before the security guard stepped back into the elevator. She looked at the package. It was from Nordstrom. She didn't remember ordering anything from there. Sometimes, on a whim, her mother would send her things she saw online, so it wasn't too unusual.

Emma put the package on the breakfast bar. A glass of wine was in order. After all, she deserved it. She took the package and the wine to the living room and flopped on the couch almost spilling her wine. "Okay, what does Mom think I need this time?" she whispered as she tore open the package.

She nearly fell off the couch when she pulled out the contents. Inside the box was a black lace open cup bralette that would barely cover anything and a matching thong with garter belt. The computer-generated note inside said, "To help turn trash into a treasure."

Emma dropped the box, which toppled the wine glass, spilling its contents onto the floor. Suddenly it was hard for her to breathe and the room was spinning. This was icing on the cake after this afternoon. She still didn't understand why someone would want to torment her.

She immediately reached for her cell to call Hunter, but then put the phone down. After today's display, she realized that was no longer an option. She was on her own and didn't like this feeling. This was a merry-go-round ride she desperately wanted to get off. Bile rose in her throat. but she managed not to empty what little was in her stomach. She grabbed the back of the couch for support until the room stopped spinning.

When she finally composed herself, Emma decided to play amateur detective and called Nordstrom. Once she connected to the right department, she asked, "Hi. I just received a delivery from your store that I didn't order. It looks like it was a gift but there wasn't any name on the card. I would very much like to thank the person who sent it and was hoping that you might be able to provide me with that information." Emma tried to sound calm.

"Sure. Let me see if I can pull up the order. Can you provide me with your name and address?" Emma gave the woman on the other end of the phone the information as calmly as she could muster. "Oh, I see the order. I'm sorry, though. The transaction was done in cash at one of our Boston-area stores. I hope that the merchandise was to your satisfaction."

"Yes, the merchandise was very nice. Thank you for checking." Emma disconnected, still rattled. She thought about calling Ryan but decided against it. She realized she didn't reset the alarm from when she came home earlier in the day. Once the alarm was set, she felt more secure. Her phone rang, almost giving her a heart attack. Emma's brother's image popped up on caller ID and Emma chose to ignore the call. The last thing she needed was to hear more about her brother's sexcapades. She made a mental note to call him later that weekend.

Emma headed to the trash can with the 'gift' and then stopped herself. What if she was murdered and this was evidence? "OMG! I watch way too much TV!" she screamed. "But just in case, I'll put it in the spare bedroom closet," she whispered. She was thankful that she hadn't turned on the cameras so that the security guys weren't seeing her mini-manic episode.

Emma realized that her spilled wine had fully soaked into the area rug in the living room. "Just perfect!" she said to herself. For the next hour she moved the furniture around so that she could lift the rug to dry the hardwoods underneath. As she was cursing to herself, thoughts of Hunter and the mystery woman swarmed her head. She was about to explode with fury when her phone chimed indicating there was a new text message.

Emma got off her hands and knees to grab her phone on the kitchen counter. She didn't recognize the number and debated whether to even open it. Curiosity had won the internal battle and caught Emma off-guard once again. The text was to the point, "I'll enjoy watching you wear my gift." Emma's hands started to shake. She dropped the phone on the floor. Tears started to stream down her face as she sank to the floor hugging herself. It was then that she truly realized she was alone in this. No one was going to ride in on a white horse and save her, especially not Hunter.

CHAPTER 25

———

Emma didn't know how long she had been in a fetal position on her kitchen floor. It could have been minutes or hours. A sudden pounding on the door startled her back to reality. She vaguely could make out voices in the hallway—mostly shouting either at each other or to her inside. It was like she was paralyzed. No matter how hard she tried to lift herself off the floor, she couldn't muster the energy.

The door burst open and several large men stormed the apartment. Emma still couldn't focus, even when one of the men scooped her off the floor and carried her to her bedroom. Evil images flashed through her head of what was about to happen. All she could do was sob and hoped that the end came quickly.

A blanket was draped over her as her head was placed on her pillow. The man watched her for a minute before closing the door and heading back to the main living area. Emma hadn't realized she had fallen asleep until she looked at the clock: 1:17 a.m. Her body felt achy and stiff. She could feel the salt on her cheeks from her dried tears. She sprung out of bed, remembering the events from several hours earlier.

She was still wearing the same clothes she'd had on when she came home on Friday night. Nothing hurt or was disturbed in places it shouldn't be. Emma surmised that whoever moved her to her bed was not someone wishing to harm her. She cautiously opened the door and peered down the hallway. All seemed quiet and still. She could see the living room lights were on and possibly the TV.

She thought that she was being quiet sneaking into the living room until a voice from the couch said, "Glad to see that you got some rest." Emma's pulse returned to a normal pace as she recognized Ryan's voice.

"Did you carry me to my bedroom?" Emma tried to grasp the events of the evening.

"Sure did, sweetheart. You were in *no* condition to do it yourself. How do you feel?"

"Like I got sucker punched. I could hear voices and saw shadows but couldn't seem to focus. How did you know I needed help?" Emma was perplexed and visibly rattled.

"The one thing I forgot to tell you, and I mean I *truly* forgot, was that I also installed a tracking device of sorts in your phone." Emma visibly tensed at the thought of this, which Ryan immediately picked up on. "Emma, this is all for *your* safety. And, honestly, after tonight I'm glad that I did it. It's like the one in Hunter's cars that shows the location of your phone 24/7. The added feature, and the one that got me to break the sound barrier getting over here last night, is that it sends me an alert if anyone not in your contact list calls, emails, or texts you. If it's a text or email, I also get a copy."

Emma was dumbfounded but let Ryan continue. "The text you received was from a blocked number on a burner cell. That immediately sent off warnings in my head. Once I saw the text, I knew I had to get over here in a flash. Look, please don't be mad at me. Your safety was my main concern." Ryan paused to give Emma time to absorb this.

After a few minutes of silence, Emma walked over to where Ryan was standing and hugged him. Neither said a word, they just stood there holding each other. Ryan broke the moment and looked at Emma. "I was worried you were really going to be pissed off at me. This was not a reaction I had anticipated." Both stood looking at each other, realizing they were standing so close to one another they could hear the other's heartbeat.

Ryan stepped away first to regain his composure. It was not like him to get wrapped up in a moment. Emma was Hunter's girlfriend and completely off-limits, he reminded himself. Ryan was used to being in dangerous situations but always shielded himself from romantic entanglements. He knew that he shouldn't be having the feelings stirring inside him.

"Emma, I need to see the package that was sent to you," Ryan said flatly.

"It's in the spare bedroom closet on the top shelf." Emma shook her head as she remembered what was in the package.

Ryan was secretly thankful to go to another part of the condo as it felt like the walls were closing in on him, being so close to Emma. He made a mental note that as soon as this situation was resolved, he'd call one of his go-to dates and work off some adrenaline. Ryan had a myriad of women at his beckon and call—all of them trying to "fix" him into the settling down type. He knew he was being a rascal, but they never complained.

Ryan returned to the living room with the box in hand. He placed it on the coffee table in front of both of them.

"Ryan, I probably should tell you that I did some sleuthing of my own after I opened the package."

Ryan cocked an eye at Emma.

"I called Nordstrom and told them that the card didn't come with a name on it, and I wanted to thank the person who sent it."

"What did they tell you?" Ryan was impressed with Emma's initiative.

"They said that it was paid for in cash at one of their Boston-area stores but that was all they knew. So that was a dead-end, I guess."

"Not necessarily. Now we know that this person is in this area. If it was done over the internet, then the person could be anywhere in the world."

"I don't know which is worse. It's creepy to know that at any time I could be next to this person on the subway, in a store, or walking down the street."

"Do you mind if I take this with me?"

Emma shook her head.

"I am going to see if my team can look at any of the store's surveillance footage in the area around the time this was purchased. If this guy was smart, he probably sent a decoy in to do his bidding for him, but you never know."

"Thanks, Ryan." Emma wanted to ask if Hunter knew any of this but decided that she really didn't want to know.

Ryan grabbed the package and his jacket as he headed towards the door. "Make sure the alarm is set, and I'll let you know what I find out - if anything." Ryan left as fast as he could to make sure there were no mixed signals between them.

The ride down the elevator gave Ryan time to make a plan of his next steps, including which of his lovely ladies to ply with his devilish charms for the next few hours. Ryan finally decided as he walked out to his car that the only one who could handle all this pent-up frustration was Alexa. Ryan licked his lips as he imagined the role-playing and bondage that Alexa was in for.

The text message kept running through Emma's head like a song lyric she couldn't get rid of. Someone was watching her. Had this person been watching her since this whole thing started? Emma knew she'd drive herself crazy thinking of hypotheticals. She poured herself a stiff drink. Hopefully, it would put her to sleep and push these thoughts out of her head.

When Emma finally fell asleep, it was a restless sleep. Her subconscious wasn't playing fair; thoughts of the lingerie, Hunter, and Ryan danced around. She fell deeper into a slumber as Ryan overtook her thoughts. His rock-solid muscles holding her against him as she could feel the twinges of desire flow through them.

CHAPTER 26

———

Emma finally resurfaced around 9 a.m. as a splinter of sunlight snuck through the drapes. As she stretched to wake up her stiff body, last night's events vividly played out in her mind like a movie. Suddenly, Emma broke into laughter. She was laughing so hard that her eyes began to water and her ribs hurt. All she could think of what how crazy this all was. Sure, she was successful—but not in the Logan success category. She was what she thought of as naturally pretty—but not in the super-model kind of way. In the big scheme of the universe, she was probably slightly above average… so why had this creep targeted her? That was the million-dollar question that would solve this mystery, she pondered.

The rest of the weekend was relatively uneventful. Sunday brunch with Morgan and Hannah was mostly low-key, except for the two bottles of champagne they finished off. Emma, who never kept any secrets from her best friends, decided not to mention the recent happenings. Partly because if she said them out loud, it would make them even more real. And partly so that her best friends wouldn't be put in any danger.

After brunch, the trio opted to head to the North End for some genuine cannolis. While at the bakery, each of them decided to load up on pastries to take to their respective workplaces. The day was bright and warm with the birds chirping. Normally, Emma would have walked home from the bakery. Today she decided taking a cab was the safer choice, but it pained her to know that her life had already changed as a result of all this craziness.

As she got out of the cab in front of her building, she noticed people were going about their business on a beautiful Sunday. To them, this was another typical weekend spent with family and friends. Once inside the lobby, she noticed the two security guards manning the front desk. Both nodded in her direction and went back to looking at the monitors in front of them. She wondered if these were the men who helped Ryan on Friday night but wasn't about to ask. The quicker she could forget that night all the better.

When the elevator doors opened, a faint hint of Versace Pour Homme cologne filtered out. There was only one person she knew who wore that brand. The champagne's effects were starting to wear off causing Emma's pulse to elevate slightly at the thought of her guest.

The doors opened to a quiet apartment and the hint of the cologne. She heard the floor behind her creak ever so slightly. She spun around to see Hunter standing in front of her with his hands in the pockets of his Lucky Brand jeans. For the next few seconds they stared like they were sizing each other up.

"I realize that you own the building, but you are invading my privacy showing up unannounced." Emma glared at Hunter as if challenging him to pick a fight.

"Ryan told me what happened on Friday night."

Emma had at least one question answered in that Ryan was still reporting back to Hunter.

"I won't tell you how disappointed I was to learn of this latest episode from Ryan and not you."

"Well, Hunter, we all know how extremely busy you are with business these days. Your influencing and negotiating skills are getting a real workout." Emma seethed.

Hunter couldn't hide his bewilderment at Emma's comments. "I'm not exactly sure where you are going with this, Emma. If you have something to say, just say it." Hunter was chillingly calm, like a predator before the kill.

"It's not even worth getting into. As you can see, I'm perfectly fine. I survived another day and plan on continuing to do so. Now, if you'll excuse me, I have some work to catch-up on. I believe you know your way out." Emma strutted to her home office and left Hunter standing in the foyer. She had to admit that it felt good to have the upper hand in that conversation.

When she heard the faint sound of her front door closing, she emerged from her office to a silent apartment. A pang of disappointment washed over her at the thought that Hunter hadn't even tried to find out why Emma was acting so cold towards him. A sign that he was indeed preoccupied with someone else, in Emma's mind. As she looked around the empty apartment, she noticed a note on the island in the kitchen.

The handwritten note was on Hunter's personal stationary and read, "Don't believe everything you see or hear." Emma stared at the note and knew that it was indeed Hunter's handwriting but had no idea what he was trying to tell her.

About the Author

Tracey Ryan grew up in central Massachusetts, where she currently resides with her husband. She holds an undergraduate degree in marketing and an MBA, which has led to a successful career in financial services marketing for over twenty years. She has been a devoted mystery reader and an avid writer for most of her life.

———

Visit TraceyLRyan.com
for more information about the
author including tour dates.

Made in United States
North Haven, CT
06 July 2023

38638955R10137